Table of Contents

Mail Order Bride: Love, Honor & Keep Her
A Sweet Historical Western Romance
Faithful Mail Order Bride Series
Copyright © 2015 by Rose Dumont

Mail Order Bride: Love, Honor & Keep Her
CHAPTER ONE

Southeastern Montana, 1896

Grayson Lee got off his horse, tied it to the rail and with a quick stumbling step, walked into the post office. Tall and lean, work on the ranch had made Grayson muscular, his wavy brown hair kissed gold by the sun. His silver-blue eyes were piercing, yet kind.

"Mornin' Grayson." Dale Henderson stood behind the desk, sorting mail.

"Morning' Dale. Anything for—"

"No need to ask, I'm already looking," he smirked. Dale peered through his bifocals as he thumbed through the short stack of mail. "Yep, here ya go." He handed the letter over to Grayson. "Must be something special inside, eh?"

"You have no idea!" Grayson exited the post office with a big smile, the envelope held up to his nose as he closed his eyes and smelled the sweet perfume. He ripped open the paper and leaned against the railing.

Dear Grayson,
Yes! I will marry you. I've already made plans and will be arriving on the last Friday of the month on the Laurel Springs Stage. I look forward to seeing you in person and starting the rest of our lives together. You are a dream come true.
Devotedly yours,
Charlotte

Grayson had been exchanging letters with Charlotte for several months. His late wife, Laura, had died in childbirth, leaving him alone to raise their daughter, who was now almost three. He'd never considered marrying again, until he realized that Jenni needed a mother. The local pickings were slim as far as good marrying-type women, so with great trepidation he decided to place an ad in the Matrimonial Times:

A YOUNG MAN, 25, 6 FEET 2 INCHES, WEIGHING 180 POUNDS, STRONG, OF FAIR FEATURES and owner of a thriving cattle ranch would like to hear from a young lady from 18–25 who seeks a good home and kind husband. Must be affectionate, able to cook and clean and willing to help me raise my three-year-old daughter. Address, confidentially, Box 3, Laurel Springs Post Office, Montana.

Grayson hadn't expected many replies; there were so many men for women to choose from who weren't previously married and didn't already have a child. But a lovely woman by the name of Charlotte had answered. She said she loved children and would love to help raise his daughter. Grayson was especially happy to see her say that. He just wanted a loving companion who would also love his Jenni.

Grayson hadn't told a soul about his correspondence with his bride-to-be. He didn't want anyone to know until he knew for sure she would marry him. He would no doubt be teased by his younger brother, Jarrod. Jarrod and Grayson took over the 100,000 acre ranch after their father, James, died of a heart attack five years ago. The brothers felt he died more so of a broken heart after his wife, their mom Mary, died a year earlier of consumption.

When Grayson got married, Jarrod moved out of the main house and built a second small cabin for himself on the ranch. There was more than enough land as well as plenty of space for a married couple with a child and a single brother to all live. Now Grayson had to tell Jarrod and, more importantly, make sure everything was perfect for Charlotte's arrival.

CHAPTER TWO

Grayson was just finishing up eating breakfast with Jarrod when he thought it was a good time to tell his brother about Charlotte. "I'm a lucky man, Jarrod."

"Why's that? Did you get that splinter out of your finger finally?" Jarrod smirked at Grayson while finishing his last bite of food off his plate.

"Ha, ha. No. it's much more than that." Grayson hesitated. "I... I..."

Jarrod threw down his napkin, leaned back in his chair and stared at his brother. "What? Spit it out."

"I'm getting married." Grayson felt an instant sigh of relief once the words left his mouth.

"Married? To who? I've never even seen you with any woman since Laura."

"Her name is Charlotte. I've been writing to her for several months and now she's coming out to be with me in two weeks."

"Is she one of them mail-order brides?" Jarrod asked.

"I guess you could say that, but she's much more than that to me. She's sweet, beautiful and wants to be with me and Jenni."

"How do you know she's beautiful?"

Grayson pulled out a photo from his vest pocket and showed it to Jarrod.

"Whoooo-wheeee!" Jarrod grabbed the photo from Grayson to get a better look. "She sure is pretty, IF that's her real photo."

"Of course it is." Grayson quickly grabbed the photo back.

"Well does she have a sister?" Jarrod asked with raised brows and a smile.

"No. No sister. She's an only child." Grayson took another look at Charlotte's photo before he slipped it back into his vest pocket.

"Darn. Well, I'll be happy for ya when I see her."

"Thanks. I guess." Grayson stood up from the table. "I have to start cleaning up before she arrives."

"I thought that's what SHE's for?"

"She's not just for cleaning and besides that, I don't want to scare her away thinking I live in a pig sty."

Jarrod looked around the room. "But you *do* live in a pig sty."

"Nevermind! I just want her to feel welcome and comfortable when she arrives, that's all. And don't forget, some of this mess around here is yours."

Since Laura died, Jarrod moved back into the main house. It was easier than maintaining his cabin with a fire to keep warm, having to always carry water and making meals separate from Grayson. His cabin wasn't the nicest house either, more of a bachelor's shack. Just a quick build he put up when Grayson married Laura. He planned on making it better, but hadn't made the time to work on it.

Besides all this, Jarrod preferred staying in the main ranch house which was the complete opposite of his shack. It had a large kitchen with a wood-burning cook stove and oven alongside a smaller breakfast nook with its own fireplace. There was also a separate pantry room off the kitchen for storage.

The kitchen then led out to the main formal dining room, which had one long table for entertaining guests. There was also a reading room with another larger stone fireplace that covered one entire wall. Upstairs were four large bedrooms. The master bedroom had its own private balcony that overlooked one of the grazing meadows.

Their house was the largest home in all of Laurel Springs. James Lee, their father, had done well in silver mining and selling lumber off his land, and had built up a fine herd of cattle to sell nearly every year since the ranch had been established.

"Yeah, yeah, yeah. Well, you're my brother and I'll be glad to help you out. I know it's been hard these last few years without Laura and raising Jenni by yourself. I'll be happy for you if this is what you want."

"Yes, it is."

"I'll clean up any of my mess, but don't get to thinking I'm gonna pick up your dirty socks off the floor or something like that. But I'll help you out and tend to your ranch chores while you fix up the place for... for... What's her name again?"

"Charlotte."

"Yeah, Charlotte."

"Thanks, Jarrod. I appreciate it. It'll be good to have a woman on the ranch again. Something just ain't quite right without one."

"Sure will be nice to have home-cooked meals again. And I won't even mind if she tells me to clean up first before eating."

"How considerate of you."

"Yep. You know I'm just a big softy like you," Jarrod chuckled.

"Get outta here, ya big fool!" Grayson picked up a dish rag and threw it at Jarrod as he laughed and walked out the door.

***

Grayson worked for about an hour cleaning up the cabin, but then realized all he had done was moved things around and made lots of little piles. Clothes here, tools there, but nothing was really organized.

WELL, AT LEAST YOU CAN WALK AROUND WITHOUT STUBBING YOUR TOE ON SOMETHING, Grayson thought to himself. I THINK I'LL LET CHARLOTTE FIGURE OUT WHERE EVERYTHING SHOULD GO. SHE'LL LIKE THAT, FEELING NEEDED AND ALL. YEAH. IT'S PERFECT. Grayson felt good about his cleaning effort and moved on to fixing some lunch.

The loud thump and clanging of the skillet and coffee cup falling off the counter woke up Jenni in the next room and made her cry, "Wu wu wouaaaaaaaaaaa!"

"Now I did it." Grayson shook his head. "Hold on, Jenni. Daddy's coming." Grayson went into the next room and picked up Jenni from the crib. "It's okay." Grayson hugged her and then made a funny face and tickled her belly. "Are you hungry?"

Jenni looked up at Grayson with her hand in her mouth and tears rolling down her cheeks and slowly shook her head yes.

"I'm hungry too, so let's get something to eat."

Grayson carried Jenni into the kitchen and sat her in the chair. He then made her porridge and fried up a couple of partridge breasts from yesterday's hunt for himself.

"How's that porridge? Good?" Grayson shook his head up and down at Jenni.

Jenni held tightly onto the lower third of her spoon, dug into her porridge and then directed it as best she could towards her mouth. Most of it arrived in her mouth while the rest dripped down her chin and onto the table.

"Well, at least three-fourths of a spoonful is better than nothing." Grayson smiled, thinking how nice it was going to be to have Charlotte here with him and his daughter. He loved Jenni and taking care of her more than anything else, but knew it would be a big relief to have Charlotte caring for her too. He knew that nothing could really replace the love of a mother, not even the love of a father.

Because Grayson had to run the ranch, he couldn't always be home to take care of Jenni. He had an old friend of the family, Miss Jean, who offered to look after her for him. She was widowed and had no children of her own. She lived by herself and, at first, Grayson would pick her up, bring her back to the ranch and then take her home everyday. But then one day while dropping her off at her home, he asked her to stay.

"Miss Jean, how about you just staying at our ranch?"

"For how long?"

"As long as you like. It will be a lot easier on the both of us and better for Jenni. She loves you and is sad every time you leave."

"Well, if you put it that way, I guess I could stay with y'all. I actually get kind of lonely at home with no one around, and my old bones are getting tired of this bumpy ride twice a day. So, yes. I accept your invitation."

"Great! Just pack your things and I'll pick you up tomorrow."

Miss Jean had been with them for nearly three years and had been a blessing in their life. But now at age 71, she was aging fast and becoming frailer. Her joints ached most of the time, and she wouldn't be able to take care of Jenni for much longer. Charlotte couldn't be coming into their lives at a better time.

Up until last year, Miss Jean would do all the women's work in the house in addition to looking after Jenni. But Grayson saw that she was getting more and more tired and in pain by the end of the day, so told her to stop cleaning and cooking.

At first, she resisted, but eventually her body's physical limitations overrode her will and spirit. She could still look after Jenni, put her to sleep, be there when she woke up and feed her, but now Grayson had to help out more. However, he definitely felt better that someone was always home with Jenni.

CHAPTER THREE

With Miss Jean's help, as well as a wide assortment of opinions and input from the local women in town, Grayson was able to make plans for a beautiful wedding that he hoped would impress Charlotte. He spared no expense. The ceremony would be at the church followed by an outdoor reception at his ranch with lots of flowers, decorations and food and drink for all his guests. He was so excited and happy. He nearly invited the whole town minus the saloon ladies, town drunk, and any other unsavory characters who might cause trouble.

"Is there anything else you think I should do for the wedding, Miss Jean?"

"I think you've done it all, short of having a diamond-studded carriage drawn by unicorns." Miss Jean smirked.

"I just want to make it perfect for her. She deserves the best."

"I'm sure she'll love it all and if she doesn't, well, she's not the girl for you. You shouldn't have to go through all of this to impress her. She should love you and want to marry you if all you did was get married at the feed store."

"Yes, I know. And I have no doubt she would still marry me without all this extra fuss. I just want to make it special for her, that's all."

"No doubt you have."

"And there's something I'd like to say to you before she arrives."

"Yes?"

"I just want you to know that I am forever grateful to you for looking after Jenni for me. I don't know what I would have done without you."

"I'm sure you would have found a way, but I'm glad I was able to be there for you and Jenni. You and our family go way back so you are, of course, like family to me. I never thought twice about being there for you and Jenni after Laura passed."

Grayson hugged Miss Jean and gave her a big kiss on the cheek.

"Oh, stop. You know I don't like getting all soft and sentimental about things."

"Yes, Miss Jean," Grayson said with a big smile, and gave her another hug.

"Now I don't expect you or Charlotte to want an old lady in the house, so I guess I'll be moving back to my house since it's still standing there empty. But I'd like to still have regular visits to see Jenni. I sure will miss seeing her everyday."

"What? Don't talk such foolishness. You ain't going nowhere. This house is plenty big for all of us. Charlotte knows how important you are to me and Jenni, and we wouldn't have it any other way. You're staying, Miss Jean, and that's all there is to it."

"Well, if you insist."

"I do."

"Alright then. I guess I'm staying." Miss Jean paused and then looked directly at Grayson. "Thank you, Grayson."

"No need to thank me. Like you, I never thought twice about it." Grayson grabbed his hat from the rack and headed out the door. "I'll be back later around supper time. I've got to help Jarrod fix a fence line that's been busted up on the south end. See ya, Miss Jean."

"See ya, Grayson. Me and Jenni will hold down the fort."

"I know you will." Grayson winked and closed the door behind him.

***

Grayson got on his beloved horse, Buck, and rode out to Jarrod at the other end of the ranch. His horse was a stout buckskin gelding standing almost fifteen hands high with the same reddish-tan color as a mule deer's summer coat. His mane and tail were black as were all four legs beginning just above each knee all the way down to the black hooves.

The horse was born on the ranch eleven years earlier from a mare and stallion that had been captured from a wild herd near their ranch. Grayson had taken an interest in the colt when he first saw it in the pasture and it was the first horse he broke and trained completely by himself. There were times he regretted they had gelded the horse, but knowing how hard his sire was to handle, he knew it was the practical thing to do. As a gelding, he was a calm working horse that Grayson could always depend upon.

It was a warm day, with a slight breeze that ruffled the wildflowers and sage, which perfumed the air. The sky was deep blue with a few white, puffy clouds. Grayson took in a deep breath, enjoying his slow ride and thinking about Charlotte and how happy he was. He thought about the two of them one day in the future enjoying a picnic out in the same wildflower patch under the blue sky and warming sun.

From a distance, Jarrod could see Grayson sauntering slowly over the hill toward him. WHAT'S TAKING HIM SO LONG? HE'S MOVING AS SLOW AS WINTERTIME MOLASSES, Jarrod thought to himself.

Finally Grayson made it up to Jarrod and got off his horse.

"Hey day-dreamer, what took you so long? You looked like a fair maiden taking her horse for a Sunday stroll." Jarrod took off his hat and wiped the sweat from his brow. "This fence isn't gonna fix itself, ya know."

"Sorry I'm late. I talked to Miss Jean longer than I expected and got over here as quickly as I could."

"Quickly? If Buck was walking any slower he'd be going backwards."

"Alright, alright. Well, I'm here now. I see you got this corner covered. I'll head on down to the other end where it's busted and work towards you."

"Sounds good to me. So what did you talk to Miss Jean for so long about?"

"I just wanted her to know that I'm grateful for what she's done for me and Jenni all these years. And to know that she doesn't have to leave when Charlotte and I get married."

"You want her to stay?"

"Of course. She has nowhere to go but that lonely, empty house of hers. She has no other family but us."

"Does Charlotte know she's staying?"

"Well, I didn't exactly come around to telling her that, but she knows how important Miss Jean is to us. I'm sure she won't mind."

"I wouldn't assume nothing, but that's on you. Women are funny sometimes, and Charlotte might think Miss Jean won't respect her as being the woman of the house or something like that."

"Don't be silly. Miss Jean and Charlotte will get a long just fine. She's like a grandmother to Jenni and that's what she'll continue to be."

"Well, I hope so 'cause I sure do like Miss Jean and even though she's getting older and hasn't been able to cook us meals like she used to, like you said, I feel she's family to us."

"I'm glad you think more of her than just being a cook for us," Grayson smirked.

"Of course. Don't twist up my words. You know what I meant."

"Yes, Jarrod. I do. Anyway, let's get this fence finished. Charlotte will be arriving in just a few days and I don't want to be out here fixing fences when she comes."

"You know we're gonna have to fix fences long after Miss Charlotte arrives. She knows you're a rancher, right?"

"Yes, of course. I'm just saying the day before the wedding I don't want to be out here. I got a lot of stuff planned and need to make sure everything goes right."

"Gosh, you act like the President is coming to town."

"She's much more important to me than the President."

"Well, Miss Jean and those other women from town will help you. I guess I'll help you too. But you better believe I'm not hanging ribbons or decorating with doilies or fringy things. I'll help with moving around tables or heavy stuff though."

"Fringy things?"

"I don't know what those things are called that ladies decorate with. But you get my drift."

"Thanks, Jarrod. Any help would be much appreciated."

"So let's get this fence fixed then, eh?"

"Yep. I'm on it."

Grayson and Jarrod worked on the fence for a few hours, meeting at the middle of the mend where they gathered up their tools, put them in their saddle bags and then mounted their horses. The sun was just going down behind the mountains in the distance.

"I told Miss Jean we'd be home around supper time. She was going to start a beef stew for us and maybe bake some biscuits, so it should be ready when we get there."

"Sounds good to me. I'm starving."

Grayson took off with Buck into a full gallop yelling, "First one home gets the extra biscuit!"

Jarrod kicked his horse and tried to catch up with his brother. "Oh, sure. Now when there's food involved you're in a hurry!"

CHAPTER FOUR

Charlotte stepped off the stagecoach and looked through the crowd. Then their eyes met. Grayson waved and Charlotte waved back. He hurriedly weaved through the crowd until finally they were both standing in front of each other.

"Hello, Miss Charlotte. I sure am glad to see you."

Charlotte Abbey Chadwick stood tall at five foot nine inches. She was slender, yet curvaceous. She had long, flowing, golden-bronze hair that was tied back in a bun. She had a warm complexion, shimmering sapphire-blue eyes, a petite nose and full pink lips. Grayson knew she was beautiful from her photo, but after seeing her in person he felt the photo did not do her justice.

"Did you think I might not come?"

"The thought did cross my mind. You're just so beautiful and it's such a long way for you to come and be with me."

"I love you, Grayson. It's why I'm here and why I want to marry you."

"I love you too, Charlotte, and I can't wait to marry you. Here, let me take your bags and get you to your hotel room. I made sure they reserved the best room for you."

"Sounds good to me. It's been a long trip, and I would love to get cleaned up and have a good night's rest."

"Oh, these are for you." Grayson handed Charlotte a bouquet of daisies, her favorite flower.

"How kind of you. They're beautiful."

"Your favorite, right?"

"Uh, oh, yes. My favorite. Daisies."

They made the short walk to the Laurel Springs Hotel. Grayson checked Charlotte in and then carried her bags to the room.

"Is the room okay?"

"Yes, this will be fine."

"Good. Well, I'll let you get settled in and get a good night's rest. I'll swing by in the morning so we can have breakfast together."

"Okay. I'll see you in the morning, then. Goodnight, Grayson."

"Goodnight, Charlotte." Grayson shut the door. "Make sure you lock the door," Grayson instructed from the hallway. He waited a few seconds and then heard the door lock.

"All secure," Charlotte declared from inside the room. Charlotte was happy to see Grayson, but was exhausted from her long journey across the country. All she wanted to do was wash up and lie down and go to sleep on a soft, comfortable bed.

Grayson walked back down the stairs into the hotel foyer.

"Grayson, you're one lucky man," said Sid, the hotel desk clerk.

"I know it, Sid. And in just a couple days she'll be my wife, Mrs. Grayson Lee." He leaned on the edge of the front desk, gazed upstairs towards Charlotte's room and said, "And I can't believe she's all mine."

"Looks like it to me. You sure she's not after your money, right?"

Grayson looked back at Sid with a furrowed brow. "No, Sid. She's not like that. She would love me if I all I had was a shack and a mule."

"Well, I hope so. I've heard stories about some of these mail order brides. They marry you and then before you know it, you haven't a penny to your name."

"Not my Charlotte. She's different."

"I'll have to take your word. Only time will tell. I do wish you the best."

"You're coming to the wedding, right?"

"I'll be there. Wouldn't miss a big thing like that in our little ol' town. The ladies' gossip circle say it's gonna be a quite a fancy one."

"Are you part of the ladies' circle?" Grayson chuckles.

"Naw. I just overhear things, that's all."

"Well, I gotta get some shuteye. I'll be back in the morning for breakfast. See ya, Sid."

"Goodnight."

Grayson got on his horse and rode home under the moonlit sky. He thought about Charlotte and how happy he was to see her. He would have stayed and talked with her all night, but knew she needed the rest. He couldn't wait until morning when he could see her again.

***

Grayson barely slept a wink. His mind couldn't stop thinking about Charlotte, the wedding and how much his life was about to change. It was only four in the morning, but he decided to get out of bed since all he was doing was tossing and turning, with no sleep in between.

He started a pot of coffee and then went outside to the chicken coop to get some eggs. When he came back inside, Miss Jean was mixing up a batch of biscuits and frying bacon.

"Did I wake you up, Miss Jean?"

"I sleep pretty lightly these days, so the faintest noises wake me up. I came down and saw you through the window going to the chicken coop, so I figure you were fixing breakfast. I reckon bacon and biscuits will go with your eggs?"

"Yes, Ma'am! Thank ya. Sorry I woke you up, though."

"What are you doing up this early anyhow?"

"I couldn't sleep, thinking about Charlotte and all."

"You sure are love-struck, aren't you?"

"I'm in love, that's for sure. And as happy as can be."

"Well, you know everything isn't going to be all nice and easy with smiles all the time. I'm sure there going to be some adjusting and getting used to things for all three of ya."

"Yeah, I know Miss Jean. I'm going to make the transition as easy as I can for her AND Jenni."

"Did you give her the ring last night?"

"I was planning on it, but it was so late, and it didn't feel right giving it to her off the stage or at the hotel room. I want it to be more special than that, so I'll be taking her somewhere nice after breakfast and then give it to her there."

"Where?"

"I haven't decided yet. But it'll be nicer than the hotel room, I know that much."

CLOMP, CLOMP, CLOMP. Jarrod came down the stairs dragging his feet. His hair was messy, hanging in his eyes, and his shirt was halfway tucked into his pants. "What in the world are y'all doing down here so early? For goodness sakes, even the roosters are still sleeping and so should I."

"Sorry, Jarrod. I couldn't sleep and then I woke up Miss Jean making coffee, so she came down to help with breakfast. You hungry?"

"It was the smell of bacon that finally got me out of bed. So yeah, I'm hungry. Why can't you sleep?"

"Just thinking 'bout stuff."

"What stuff? Wait, let me guess. Charlotte, right?"

"Yeah."

"Women. They mess with your mind like that. For now, I'm glad I don't have one on my mind."

"But one day you will and you'll love every moment of it."

"We'll see. But enough talk about women. Let's get to eating."

Eventually Jenni woke up too and joined them. "Hey sleepy head. Ready for some breakfast?" Grayson picked up Jenni from her crib and brought her to the table and fed her some breakfast.

Grayson, Miss Jean and Jarrod sat around the table talking until the sunrise, reminiscing about old times with their parents and growing up on the ranch.

"Well, I've enjoyed spending this early morning with you, Miss Jean. Thanks for the breakfast and your company."

"What about MY company?" Jarrod asked.

"You're not company. You're my brother. We're pretty much always hanging out together, so nothing different there."

"I reckon."

"Anyway, I gotta get going. I told Charlotte I'd meet her for breakfast."

"You're gonna eat again?" asked Miss Jean.

"Yeah, by the time I ride into town I could be hungry again. I'm a growing boy."

"You'll be growing outward, not upward, if you keep eating like that. A boy you are not anymore."

"I'll keep that in mind, Ma'am. Maybe I'll only have two eggs, two bacon strips and two biscuits."

"Well, don't starve yourself, now," Miss Jean said with a smirk.

"No, Ma'am." Grayson winked, put on his hat and opened the front door. "Oh, and Jarrod. I'll be with Charlotte most of the day, showing her around and stuff. If you need me, then I'll be either in town or here at the house."

"So when am I and Miss Jean gonna meet this Charlotte of yours?"

"I figure we could have dinner together here at the ranch."

"What do you need me to do?" said Miss Jean.

"Nothing. I'll be taking care of everything. Maybe you can just help set the table for me, all pretty like with flowers or something?"

"Yes, I can certainly do that. But what about the cooking?"

"I've got it covered."

"Well, alright. But a woman from the East might be expecting more than biscuits and gravy, ya know."

"Don't worry, Miss Jean. I'll do better than that."

Grayson went out the door, hitched up the wagon to Buck and headed into town.

CHAPTER FIVE

Grayson pulled up the wagon to the hotel, engaged the brake and walked inside. Today he would propose to Charlotte and give her the engagement ring he sent away for a few months back. Although he wasn't one-hundred percent sure Charlotte would accept his proposal, he ordered the ring anyway in the hopes she would.

Most men couldn't afford an engagement ring, even the more affordable ones that were now commonly available by mail-order through the Sears & Roebuck Catalog. Grayson, however, always spent his money wisely and the last five years were especially good for his cattle business, so he had some extra money saved up.

Normally he would never consider spending so much money on something like jewelry, but he really wanted to do something special for Charlotte. Grayson spoke with a few of the more sophisticated women in town who knew more about jewelry and rings than he did, which was essentially nothing, and they told him he must get Charlotte a ring with a "Tiffany Setting".

A few months earlier…

"Tiffany Setting? What's that?" Grayson asked.

Victoria further explained, "It sets the diamond up on a pedestal, away from the band, allowing more light to shine through the diamond and make it sparkle. The Tiffany Company invented it about ten years ago. It's what all the girls want now."

"Well, if you say so."

"She'll love you forever. What a lucky girl."

"I'm the lucky one."

***

Grayson walked into the hotel foyer.

"Mornin', Grayson." Sid nodded towards the dining area. "Your lady just sat down at a table inside."

"Thanks, Sid."

Charlotte's back was to Grayson. He lightly touched her on her shoulder and said, "Good morning. I hope you haven't been waiting too long."

"No, not at all. I just sat down."

"Good. Are you hungry? They make a mighty fine breakfast here."

"Actually, not very. My stomach feels a little odd."

"Oh. Well, how did you sleep?"

"Not much. I guess it'll take me a few days or so to adjust being out here."

"I couldn't sleep a wink either. I'm just so excited you're here."

"Me too." Charlotte smiled at Grayson.

Bonnie, the waitress, came over to the table and asked, "So what'll it be for you two lovebirds?"

"Hey, Bonnie. I guess you've heard."

"Yep, word gets around fast around this li'l old town."

"Well, I'd like to introduce you to my fiancée, Charlotte."

"Howdy, Charlotte. What'll you have?"

"Nice to meet you, Bonnie. Um, I'm not sure."

"You've got to eat something, Charlotte," Grayson insisted. "How about a couple of flapjacks? They're always good here."

"Okay, I guess. But what are flapjacks?"

"Huh? You don't know what a flapjack is? It's a round, flat, fluffy-like cake. And then you smother it with butter and molasses."

"Oh, you mean pancakes. Yes, that'll be fine."

"Pancakes? I guess you folks back East call things differently than us out here. Anyway, bring us both an order of flapjacks, Bonnie. And two cups of coffee. You drink coffee, don't ya?"

"Yes, and we call it coffee too," Charlotte smirked.

"So it'll be two orders of flapjacks and two coffees. Thanks, Bonnie."

"Are you only going to eat a couple of pancakes? That seems not much for a man like yourself."

"Well, like I said, I couldn't sleep so I was up before dawn and Miss Jean and Jarrod and I had breakfast together. I already ate some eggs, biscuits and bacon. I actually was planning on eating more, but once I saw you I got all kinds of butterflies in my stomach, so a couple of flapjacks will do just fine."

"Oh, that makes more sense then. You had me worried thinking I was going to eat as much as a cowboy for breakfast."

"Naw, I can pack it away as good as any hard-working cowboy can." Grayson reached across the table and took Charlotte's hands in his. "Gosh, you have no idea how happy I am to finally have you here with me. You are a dream come true, Miss Charlotte."

"Oh, Grayson. You're too kind. I guess that's why I love you so much. Not only are you kind, but you're also handsome, strong, funny and so much more. I cannot wait to marry you."

"Just a few days away. I've been planning the event ever since I got your letter. I hope it will be the most beautiful wedding for you."

"I'm sure it will. You didn't have to fuss so much over me. I'd be happy even if it were just you and me and nothing else but the pastor to wed us."

"Well, it'll be much more than that. I had to make it special for my special lady."

"So what are we doing after breakfast?"

"I'm gonna take you around and show you my ranch. Then later on, we're gonna head back to the main house to have dinner with my brother, Miss Jean and Jenni."

"That sounds wonderful. I'm looking forward to meeting your family, especially Jenni, of course."

"She'll love you. I just know it."

"I hope so."

Grayson and Charlotte had their breakfast and then went outside the hotel.

"Here's the first one of the family I'd like to introduce you to." Grayson patted Buck on the head. "This is my horse, Buck. I was fourteen when he was born. Raised and trained him myself. He's just as close to me as any other family member."

"Well, hello Buck." Charlotte slowly approached the horse and gently stroked him along the side of his neck.

"I think he likes you."

"Glad I passed the first test."

"That's right!" Grayson chuckled. "Here. Let me help you up into the wagon and then we can get on our way."

Charlotte lifted up her dress with one hand while Grayson provided his hand for balance as she stepped up into the old buckboard wagon. She looked down at the seat covered in hay and dirt and paused before sitting down.

"Oh, let me sweep that off for you. I know this isn't the nicest way to get around town, especially for a lady like yourself, but it serves its purpose for me and Jarrod. I actually have been working on a nice buggy for you to travel in when needed." Grayson took his leather gloves and quickly swept the bench seat.

"Thank you. I guess I'll have to get used to all these western things. We don't travel in wagons like this back where I'm from." Charlotte tucked her dress under herself and slowly sat down.

"Yes, I reckon you will have to adjust. But I'll try to make it as easy as possible for you." Grayson sat down, took the reins and looked over at Charlotte, "Ready?"

"Yes...I think?"

Grayson steered Buck to the center of the dirt road and then shook the reins twice. There was a quick jerk as the wagon sped up by the pull of the horse. Charlotte's eyes grew big with fear as her right hand quickly rose to hold on to her hat while her left hand grabbed Grayson's right arm. "Oh my!" she said excitedly.

"Hold on, Miss Charlotte. It might get a little bumpy." Grayson smiled. He liked that she grabbed his arm.

"I won't have any trouble with holding on. You might have to tell me to let go, though."

"Never, Charlotte." Grayson looked into Charlotte's eyes and repeated, "Never will I want you to let go." Charlotte smiled and slightly relaxed her grip on Grayson, but never let go, as they headed out of town.

***

About a half mile out of town, the dirt road narrowed and became a little less smooth. "And I thought the road in town was rough." Charlotte held onto Grayson's arm a little tighter, bracing herself against the wagon's seat with the other arm. "Where exactly are you taking me? Looks like into the wild west I've heard so much about."

"I'm taking you to one of my favorite spots on our ranch that I like to go to when I'm not working. It's peaceful and pretty, just like you."

"You're just full of compliments, aren't you?"

"Shall I stop?"

"No, please continue." Charlotte smiled at Grayson and scooted a little closer to him.

Grayson looked back and replied, "Your eyes are prettier than the brilliant blue sky above us."

"And…?"

"And? Well, I can't use up all my compliments in one ride to the ranch. I got to spread them out for the rest of our lives together, you see."

"I guess I can accept that. Just don't let them fall too far and few between."

"No, Ma'am."

About twenty minutes later, Grayson pulled the wagon alongside a shimmering lake surrounded on one side by aspens and fir trees and a green lush meadow blooming with a rainbow of wildflowers.

"Why, this is a beautiful spot."

"Here, let me help you down." Grayson pulled up alongside the lake, put the brake on the wagon and then helped Charlotte down.

"Do you come here often?"

"I try to. Sometimes I come up here alone, sometimes with Jarrod. This lake is on our land, so it's nice and quiet. I'll invite friends from town every once in a while to go fishing with me here, but typically it's just me and Buck."

"I live in the city back home, so I've never gone to a place like this. The air is so fresh. It is indeed peaceful. I'm so used to people always being around. I think I'd feel kind of scared if I was out here alone."

"Well, you don't ever have to be out here alone, if you don't want to. I'll always be here with you."

"How nice." Charlotte paused and looked at Grayson. "So have you ever brought any other girls up here with you?"

"None that mattered. You're the first." Grayson took Charlotte's hand and they walked over to a flat-topped boulder. "Here, have a seat. It's my favorite sitting rock."

"What, no cushion?" Charlotte asked with raised eyebrows and a smile.

"I'll promise to pack one next time, my princess." Grayson bowed and then sat down next to Charlotte. "Charlotte, I know you've sacrificed a lot to come out here. You've left everything behind to come to a place you've never seen before just to be with me. I want you to know that I will do everything I can to make you happy. I will love you, protect you and care for you like no other man can. Aside from Jenni, you are everything to me."

Grayson got off the rock and knelt down on one knee. Charlotte put her hands over her mouth in surprise. "I know you already said that you'd marry me, but I thought it would be only right to ask you like it should be done." Grayson pulled out the ring from his vest pocket, took Charlotte's left hand and said, "Miss Charlotte Abbey Chadwick, will you marry me?"

With tears streaming down her cheeks, Charlotte leapt to her feet, put her arms around Grayson and exclaimed, "Yes!"

Grayson hugged Charlotte back tightly and then said, "Wait, let me put the ring on your finger!" Charlotte stood back as Grayson took her hand and slowly slipped the ring on her finger. "Is it too tight? 'Cause we can get it fitted better."

Charlotte extended her arm and spread her hand out in front of her admiring the ring. "It's a little big, but that's okay. It's perfect."

"Well we can fix that easy enough. Do you really like it?"

"I love it. I would have never dreamed of ever getting an engagement ring. I knew some girls back in Boston who did, but they were all marrying into very wealthy families."

"Well, my ranch is doing well and I had money saved up, and I felt like it would be a good thing to spend some of it on you."

"I feel so special!"

"That was the plan."

"When I ordered it, I asked for a special design. Look at it. It's shaped like your favorite flower." The center diamond was set slightly above eight other diamonds that formed the petals.

"Oh. Why yes. It's a…a daisy. How beautiful, Grayson. This was the perfect setting for you to ask me. And so is the ring."

"Well I'm glad you like it."

"I love it. And I love you, Grayson."

"I love you too, Charlotte. Forever and always." Grayson took Charlotte's hand and gently kissed it. "I can't wait to call you my wife."

"And you, my husband."

"Well, let's head on out of here and get back to the ranch."

"Sounds good to me. But I didn't bring a change of clothes. I'll be so dusty by the time we get there. I don't want to look like a cattle rustler when I meet your family."

"Oh, don't you worry a bit. They're used to seeing dusty folks, even women. You'll be as pretty as can be, whether covered in dust or not. And it's who you are that they want to know, not how clean you are. That didn't come out right, but you know what I mean."

"Well, if you say so. You at least have a wash basin that I can use to freshen up?"

"No, just an outhouse and the water from the cattle trough."

"What!"

"I'm just kiddin' you. Of course we have a wash basin. It'll be all yours."

Charlotte slapped him on the back of the shoulder. "I almost was gonna say take me back to town!"

"No you weren't. You'd still love me even with just a trough, wouldn't ya?"

"I guess. But eventually this woman would need my man to build me a proper bathroom."

"Yes, Ma'am." Grayson helped Charlotte back on the wagon, untied Buck and then headed back down the road over to the ranch.

CHAPTER SIX

Grayson came around the last turn in the road where the ranch could be seen in the distance below. "Whoa." He slowed the wagon to a stop. "Well, there she is. Wind River Ranch."

Charlotte looked upon the homestead, which consisted of the large two-story cabin with wrap-around roofed porch, a tall barn, corral, chicken coop, and several other outbuildings. Surrounding the buildings were meadows bordered by a dense spruce and fir forest with a wide meandering river. A split rail fence bordered the property where more than a dozen horses grazed along with a large herd of cattle. "Why, it's beautiful. Is all this yours?"

"Yep. And it's not mine. It's ours, Charlotte." Grayson shook the reins and headed down the curving switchback road. He pulled up next to the corral and then helped Charlotte out of the wagon. "There you go. Let me just unhook Buck and get him watered and fed. It'll only take a minute or two."

"Alright. I'll wait for you on the porch." Charlotte walked up to the cabin porch and sat down on one of the rocking chairs. Out of the corner of her eye, she thought she saw someone pulling back the corner of the curtains and looking at her, but then disappeared. She took a breath of the fresh mountain air and then sighed.

"Okay, let's get you inside so I can introduce you to Miss Jean and Jenni."

"And I still need to freshen up a bit before dinner."

"Yep." Grayson wiped his vest and pants and a cloud of dust plumed around him. "And so do I, I suppose." He opened the door and let Charlotte walk through first. Miss Jean was sitting at the kitchen table knitting. "Hey, Miss Jean. I'd like to introduce you to Charlotte."

"How do you do, Ma'am?" Charlotte walked over to the table and put out her hand. Miss Jean, somewhat stiff, slowly started to rise out of her chair, but Charlotte interrupted, "Oh, please don't get up on my account."

"Thank you, dear. I don't rise as fast as I used to." Miss Jean extended her hand. "A pleasure to meet you. Grayson has told me so much about you. We're glad you made it here safely. It's a long trip from where you came."

"Yes, it was. I'm so glad to finally be here. And Grayson has told me so much about you as well."

"Well don't let it scare you. I'm not THAT wicked."

"Oh, no Ma'am. Grayson had only good things to say about you."

Grayson chuckled. "She's just messing with you, Charlotte. I forgot to tell you our Miss Jean is also a jokester."

Charlotte looked puzzled for a moment and then laughed. "Oh! Well, don't I feel silly?"

"That's a good thing," Miss Jean declares.

"I think I'll fit in quite well here with you all."

"You mean y'all?"

"Yes, y'all. I guess I need some work on my western speak."

"You'll be talking like the rest of us in no time li'l lady."

"I…I reckon!" Charlotte said proudly.

Miss Jean looked at Grayson. "Yep, she seems to be a keeper."

"Forever and ever, Miss Jean."

"I guess that's what you're gonna promise each other a few days from now."

"That's right. 'Till death do us part, good or bad."

"Easier said than done sometimes." Miss Jean looked upward through her spectacles at Grayson.

"Not if you're marrying the best girl ever."

"Awwwe, you're so sweet, Grayson. You're making me blush."

"Well it's true!"

"Well your girl would be even better if she could freshen up a little. I feel as dusty as a tumbleweed."

"You can use the wash basin in my room." Grayson pointed around the corner. "Up the stairs, first room on your right."

"I'll be right back."

After Charlotte left, Miss Jean whispered to Grayson, "Are you sure she's the one?"

"Why of course! Why would you ask such a thing?"

"She seems nice enough. Maybe too nice. Like she's hiding something. I just want you to be sure."

"Sure I'm sure. I love her, and she loves me. I need nothing else."

"I don't want to cause you no fretting. But you know your momma would be just as critical about who's gonna marry her son. And since she's not here, God rest her soul, I feel I should be just as discerning. Just looking out for you, like you were my son. You might not be in blood, but you are in heart."

"Well I thank you Miss Jean for looking out for me and all, but I know Charlotte is the one for me. I wouldn't have gone through all this if I had any hesitation."

"I guess if you feel that way, then I can't say anything otherwise to you. I just want you and Jenni to be happy, that's all."

"Of course. And we will. The three of us WILL be happy together. I know it."

"Alright. I won't say another word about it."

Charlotte entered the kitchen, "Oh, I feel much better now. So where's Jenni?"

"She's still taking her nap. She'll be up before dinner though. Which reminds me, I need to get it started."

"That's something I should do, not you. I didn't think a man would do such a thing out here. Cook for a woman?"

"Well, it's not usual, but today I will. You'll have plenty of opportunities to make us dinner after we're married. I'll fix this one."

"You don't want ANY help?"

"Nope. Why don't you two sit out on the porch and get to know each other a little better."

"Are you sure you don't need any help?" asked Miss Jean.

"Nope. Go 'head. I've got it under control."

"Well, alright. But you holler if you need me."

"I will."

***

Charlotte and Miss Jean went out on the porch and sat down in the rocking chairs. "Oh, that breeze feels so nice. It's so beautiful here. The trees, the flowers, the fresh air. It's so different from where I'm from."

"Where is it you're from again?"

"Boston. Boston, Massachusetts. It's a pretty big city. Lots of people, lots of buildings. Not much open space like here."

"Sounds awful. Living out here isn't exactly easy. You gotta work hard to make a living and Grayson has done that, taking over his Father's ranch and all. But at least you've got space to do it. I don't think I'd like living elbow-to-elbow next to so many people like you say. I need some space to think and stretch."

"Yes, Ma'am. Living in a city is different. There are some advantages, though."

"Like what? And ya know, you can call me Miss Jean. You're nearly family now, and that's what the boys call me."

"Yes, Ma'am. I…I mean, Miss Jean."

"So what's so great about city livin'?"

"Well, there's lots of shops and places to eat. You can go to plays and listen to orchestras, although I haven't really done any of those things, being poor and all."

"Yeah, well, I don't think you're missing out on much. Those Yankees can have it all to themselves. It's not for me. No, I'd rather sit here on the porch and hear nothing but the birdsong."

"It is nice. I will miss some things about Boston, but I think I definitely can get used to this kind of life out here. I knew it would be different, but I didn't care. I just wanted to be with Grayson."

Charlotte's parents immigrated to America when Charlotte was only two years old. They were poor dairy farmers who wanted the opportunity and freedom America could provide for them and their children. Charlotte's mother's sister, Madeline, and her husband also came over on the same ship. They purchased some land together and built two small homes for their families.

They were doing well until a horrible accident happened one evening. Charlotte's mother, Elizabeth, fell in the kitchen, hitting her head on the cast iron stove and knocking herself unconscious. When she fell, she bumped a lantern over that shattered and started a fire.

Charlotte's father, Robert, was asleep. By the time he woke up, the fire had engulfed most of the house. It was apparent he tried to rescue Elizabeth, as they found his body laid over hers after he dragged her towards the front door. But there was too much fire and smoke and they both perished. Fortunately, Charlotte was over her Aunt's house when it happened.

Charlotte was only twelve years old when she lost her parents. Orphaned, her Aunt Madeline took her in until she was seventeen. Her Aunt already had six children and taking in Charlotte was a burden, especially since they were just scraping by on her husband's meager income.

When Charlotte moved out, she found temporary jobs, mostly as a servant, sometimes staying in boarding houses, sometimes staying in quarters provided by her employer. Now at age twenty-two with no prospects of a husband, Charlotte was more than happy to accept Grayson's proposal.

"I consider Grayson as one of my own sons. I want the best for him and he seems to think you are the best. Is it true? Do you really, with all your heart, truly love Grayson?"

"Why, of course, Miss Jean. I wouldn't be here if I even had the slightest reservation. I came a long way and left my only family, my sister, behind to be with Grayson. It wasn't easy, but I knew my heart belonged here with him and Jenni."

"Sister? For some reason I thought Grayson told me you were an only child."

"Uh, well…I mean a cousin of mine that feels like a sister to me."

"Oh. I see. Well, I'm glad you mentioned about being with Jenni too. You don't have any problem raising a child that isn't yours?"

"No, not at all. I will love her like I would my own. Because she means so much to Grayson, she already means that much to me. And I hope to have more children with Grayson so she wouldn't have to be an only child."

"You seem to have all the right answers. I don't know whether to like you or be suspicious of you."

"All my words come straight from the heart, Miss Jean. And why would you be suspicious?"

"Well, Grayson isn't your average dirt-poor sodbuster or cowpuncher out here. He and his brother have more than most and it's something that a girl might take advantage of."

"Oh no, Miss Jean. I would love Grayson even if he just had a nickel to his name. I love him for who he is, not what he has."

"There you go again, saying the right words."

"You've got to believe me. I'm here only for Grayson and for Jenni."

"Only time will tell, Missy. But for now, I guess I've got to believe you. Just know if you cross my Grayson, you better high-tail it back to that Yankee city of yours or your hide will be mine."

"Yes, Ma'am. I…I mean, Miss Jean."

"Now that that's settled, let's go save this boy from cooking. I know he's trying to impress you and all, but he doesn't know much more than boiling coffee and frying bacon. You do know how to cook, don't you?"

"Yes. In fact, I love to cook."

"Well good. I was afraid maybe you city folk don't cook."

"A few of us still do." Charlotte smiled at Miss Jean and they both walked back into the cabin.

***

"What a mess!" Miss Jean looked around at the flour scattered about the sink and floor. "How could you have made such a mess in such a short amount of time?"

"I don't know. I'm just trying to follow some recipes from Mrs. Wilcox."

"I don't think Miss Wilcox's recipe told you to throw flour all over the place."

"This is a little harder than I thought it would be."

"And that's why we've come back inside to save you, Dear."

"I can do it myself. It's just gonna take a little longer than I expected."

"Well, we've got to eat before sun-up, so just step aside and let us women take over."

"Really?"

"Really."

"I'm sorry, Charlotte. I wanted to make you something special for your first supper with us."

"That's okay. It'll still be special. And I like to cook, so why don't you go and do whatever it is you cowboys do, and Miss Jean and I will take care of dinner."

"Why, you are perfect, aren't you?"

"Oh, stop."

"Yeah, stop it," Miss Jean said rolling her eyes.

"Okay, ladies. I'll be out in the barn. Call me when it's ready." Grayson brushed the flour off his shirt and pants and then walked out the front door, leaving behind Miss Jean and Charlotte to cook.

About forty-five minutes later, Miss Jean went out on the front porch and rang the triangle. "Come and get it, Grayson!"

"Coming, Miss Jean!" Grayson shouted from the barn. A few moments later, he entered the cabin into the dining room to find a table full of food. There was fried chicken, mashed potatoes, green beans and cornbread. "Wow! I think you've ladies topped anything that I was gonna do."

"Of course."

"Is Jenni still not up from her nap?"

"No. She was pretty tired when I laid her down. But she needs to get up and eat with us now or she won't sleep through the night."

"I'll go get her." Grayson returned with the sleepy-eyed child over his shoulder. He put her down in front of him and introduced her to Charlotte. "Jenni, this is Miss Charlotte. She came a very long way by train just to see you and me. Say hello." Jenni shyly turned back around and hugged Grayson's leg, burying her head. "Oh, don't you be shy. Miss Charlotte wants to say hi to you. She's a very nice lady. Remember all the things I told you about her?" Jenni remained tightly wrapped around Grayson's leg, not acknowledging his question.

Charlotte crouched down in front of Jenni. "Hello Jenni. I'm so happy to finally meet you. Your Dad has told me a lot about you." Jenni slowly turned her head towards Charlotte, but did not release her grip from Grayson. "Do you like dolls?" Jenni slowly nodded her head yes. "Well I might have something that you may like."

Jenni went to one of her bags and returned with a small box covered in colored paper. "This is for you, Jenni. I brought it all the way across the country from Boston just for you." Charlotte reached out towards Jenni to hand her the present. Jenni finally broke her grip from Grayson and accepted the gift. She tore the paper to reveal a blonde-haired doll, wearing a colorful dress with little white shoes. "She has blonde hair just like you. Do you like her?" Jenni nodded yes.

"Say thank you to Miss Charlotte."

"Thank you."

"You're very welcome. Can I give you a hug?"

Jenni looked up at her Dad, unsure of what to do. "Give Miss Charlotte a hug. She won't bite." With doll in hand, Jenni opened her arms wide and gave Charlotte, who was still kneeling down, a big hug.

"Thank you, Jenni. I'm glad you like the doll and I hope to get a lot more hugs from you."

Jenni went back to Grayson and grabbed his leg again with her left arm while hugging the doll with her right.

"Okay, let's eat. I'm starved. Jenni put your doll down there and you can play with her later." Jenni propped her doll in an empty chair against the cabin wall and then Grayson put her up in a high chair at the table.

Everyone sat down at the table. "Would you like to say Grace?" Miss Jean asked Grayson.

"Yes, Ma'am." Grayson and everyone bowed their heads. "Bless us, O Lord, and these your gifts, which we are about to receive from your bounty. And thank you, O Lord, for the safe arrival of Miss Charlotte to our humble home. Through Christ our Lord."

Everyone replied in unison, "Amen."

"Where's that brother of yours? I told him not to be late for dinner."

"I dunno. He was gonna check on the herd at the north end. Maybe he lost track of time."

"Well, he's never late for dinner…or for breakfast…or for lunch. His stomach wouldn't allow it." Just then they heard the faint galloping of a horse, which became louder. "I bet that's him now."

Suddenly the door swung open and in came Jarrod, all dusty and sweaty looking. "Am I late?"

"We just sat down."

"Sorry, I'm late. But I sure am hungry."

"I'm sure YOU are. Wash your hands and then sit down with the rest of us."

Jarrod looked over at Charlotte and before sitting said, "Well, as pretty as you are, you must be Miss Charlotte. Nice to meet you, Ma'am."

"How kind of you. Nice to meet you, Jarrod."

"Sorry for the way I look. If I had more time, I would have changed and washed up a bit more."

"That's okay. After the dusty ride in with Grayson, I understand how you can get so dirty looking."

Jarrod laughed. "Yes, this is how the West is and how a cowboy looks most of the time." He sat down and then looked up and down the table at all the food. "Wow, I'm sure glad I came in time to eat. Did you make all this Miss Jean? 'Cause I know Grayson said he was gonna cook something, but he couldn't of made all this."

"It's actually the work of Charlotte and myself. Grayson just made a mess."

"Hey, at least I tried. More than what Jarrod would have done."

"If I had a girl like Charlotte come visit me, then I probably would try to cook too, so you can just hush. Anyway, let's stop all this talking and get to eating. Pass me the chicken!"

Grayson and Jarrod filled their plates several times with food until they couldn't eat any more. Charlotte was more lady-like in her portions along with Miss Jean whose appetite declined as she got older. Jenni finished what was given to her and then asked if she could go play with her doll.

"Alright, since you finished all your food, you may go and play." Grayson let her out of the high chair.

Jenni ran over to the doll and sat in the chair, stroking its hair, feeling the smooth satin-like dress and repeatedly taking the doll's shoes off and putting them back on. She talked to it and pretended to make it walk. It was quite apparent she loved her new toy.

"That sure was tasty, Miss Jean and Miss Charlotte. Thank you. Thank you very much." Jarrod rubbed his belly and sat back in his chair. "I could use a nap right about now."

"Well, I could use you and Grayson to help with cleaning up all this for us since we made such a big meal for you two."

"Yes, Ma'am," Jarrod replied.

"It's the least we can do. Thank you two for saving me from making dinner. I'm pretty sure it wouldn't have come out the same as yours."

"You do the ranching and I'll do the cooking from now on," Charlotte said.

"It's a deal," Grayson said with a big grin.

Charlotte and Miss Jean went out on the porch while Grayson and Jarrod cleaned up and washed the dishes. About thirty minutes later the two brothers joined the women outside. Grayson sat down next to Charlotte on the swing while Jarrod sat down at the top of the stairs.

"Isn't that the most beautiful sunset you've ever seen?" Charlotte asked.

"It sure is pretty, and we get lots of them like this out here. I bet you don't see sunsets like this back in Boston?" Grayson asked.

"No. No we don't."

"Well now you can see plenty. They're all yours to enjoy nearly every fair day."

"You mean for US to enjoy?"

"Yes, for US." Grayson moved a little closer to Charlotte and put his arm around her. She looked at him, smiled and laid her head on his shoulder. They both watched the sun slip down behind the mountains as it painted the sky with brilliant reds, oranges and purples.

CHAPTER SEVEN

Two days later, Grayson and Charlotte were ready to be married. Grayson had no doubts that this was the woman he wanted to spend the rest of his life with. And Charlotte had been waiting for this moment for a very long time. She was definitely ready to say, I DO.

Every pew in the church was occupied since Grayson had invited nearly the entire town to his wedding. Grayson stood tall and proud, wearing his finest suit and shined black shoes. His hair was slicked back and his face freshly shaved, showing off his chiseled jawline. Charlotte stood across from him, looking even more beautiful than he could have ever imagined. He was so happy to be standing there with her, his beautiful bride.

Ladies whispered compliments of Charlotte's appearance to each other. She wore a dress given to her by her last employer. The woman of the house where she had worked was very fond of Charlotte and wanted her to have a nice dress, knowing Charlotte couldn't afford one. It was an ornately beaded, cream silk satin bodice that laced at the back. The two-layered full sleeves were trimmed with lace and a full skirt flowed softly into the long train with pleated ruffle trim at the hem. She walked up the aisle, carrying a bouquet of daisies, of course.

When Grayson took Charlotte's hands in his, she trembled. He sensed her nervousness and squeezed her hands tightly for a moment to reassure her. He smiled at her, and she smiled back.

Pastor John began the wedding. "Grayson James Lee, do you take Charlotte to be your wedded wife, to live together in marriage? Do you promise to love her, comfort her, honor and keep her for better or worse, for richer or poorer, in sickness and health, and forsaking all others, be faithful only to her, according to God's holy ordinance, for as long as you both shall live?"

"I do." Grayson's answer was quick and confident.

"Charlotte Abbey Chadwick, do you take Grayson to be your wedded husband to live together in marriage? Do you promise to love him, comfort him, honor and keep him for better or worse, for richer or poorer, in sickness and health and forsaking all others, according to God's holy ordinance, be faithful only to him so long as you both shall live?"

"I do." Charlotte's voice quivered.

"By the power vested in me, I hereby pronounce you husband and wife. You may now kiss the bride."

Grayson leaned in slowly, tilting his head and gently pressing his lips to Charlotte's for a quick, but loving kiss. Loud clapping broke the silence. They both turned toward the congregation and then Grayson reached down to grasp Charlotte's hand. They smiled to everyone and quickly walked down the aisle and out of the church, where they embraced and kissed again. The buggy was waiting for them in front, adorned with streams of white ribbons.

Grayson helped Charlotte into the buggy seat and then sat down beside her. He grabbed the reins, turned to Charlotte and said, "Ready to go home, Mrs. Lee?"

"Yes, my husband!"

Grayson looked over at the gathering crowd outside the church and shouted, "Y'all meet us out at the ranch for food and drink!" Everyone waved to the new couple as they drove off down the dirt road, white ribbons trailing in the wind behind them.

***

Grayson, with the help of Miss Jean, his brother, ranch hands and neighbors, had decorated a corner field next to the stream for the after-wedding party. Tables were set up for all the guests, each with a centerpiece jar of daisies. They had gathered up some scrap wood for a makeshift stage for the local musicians to play. They had also made a flattened square area for people to dance.

As they came around the last bend to the ranch, Charlotte could see all the tables and decorations. "Did you do all that by yourself?"

"Naw, I had help. But it was all my idea. I wanted to make our wedding day special for you."

"Just saying 'I do' to me already made it special enough."

"Me too, Charlotte." Grayson gave her a peck on the cheek.

Grayson helped Charlotte out of the buggy, and then they walked to the tables. "How beautiful all the flowers are."

"Daisies. Your favorite."

"You sure do listen when I tell you something I like. I guess I'll have to let you know of my other favorite things." Charlotte smirked.

"Let me know them all. And I reckon as time goes by, and we get to know each other better, I WILL know all your favorite things."

"And I'll get to learn yours."

"Why, you and Jenni are my favorites."

"Yes, you're going to make a fine husband." They both laughed.

Grayson looked at Charlotte's fancy dress and asked, "Do you want to change into something more suitable for being outside?"

"Yes, I probably should. I just know I'll either get grass stains, mud or sauce or a combination of all on this dress. I wouldn't want to ruin it. It's so pretty."

"Yes, it is. But you're what makes it pretty. In fact, you're much more beautiful than that dress."

"If you continue to compliment me like that, we're definitely going to have a very long and happy marriage."

"Yes, there will be plenty more where that came from."

Charlotte smiled and then went to the house to change into one of her simpler dresses. It was still nice, one she would wear to church, but wouldn't worry so much about getting it dirty like she would the satin wedding gown.

When she walked out the front door to the porch, she could see a line of wagons, buggies and men on horses coming down the trail to the ranch. She was thrilled that Grayson had put together this party for their wedding celebration, but was a little nervous about meeting all these strangers from town. She didn't want them to ask her too many questions, especially about her past. But she would try her best to be accepted by them. Above all, she was relieved to finally be married to Grayson. Nothing could change that.

"Come on, Charlotte. Nearly everyone's here." Grayson waved to her from across the meadow.

Charlotte could smell the beef that was being charred on the grill over the open fire. Grayson had butchered one of his cows for the occasion. There would be steaks, smoked brisket, shredded beef and more.

Miss Jean had made some side dishes: stewed carrots, potato salad, baked beans and sweet corn pudding. Some of the other women from town were bringing more dishes and desserts: apple pies, molasses cakes, custards, turnovers and cobblers. All the food was laid out on a long table and people formed a line on each side, piling their plates high.

When it looked like most everyone had arrived, Grayson banged on the dinner triangle. "If I can have everyone's attention for a second or two." The chatter of the crowd slowly diminished until only a few children's voices were heard, followed by a "Sshh!"

"I would like to thank everyone for joining Charlotte and I today in our wedding celebration. As some of you know, it's been a tough few years since Laura's passing for me and Jenni. I thought I would never marry again. But then Charlotte came into my life and changed everything." Grayson looked over at Charlotte with adoring eyes and a smile. "Anyway, I'm not one for long speeches. I just wanted to share this happy moment in my family's life with y'all, so enjoy and eat up!" The guests all applauded along with a few hoots and hollers let out by some of the men.

After everyone ate plenty and only a few crumbs remained on the long table of food, the dance floor was cleared, and the band began to play. It was a romantic tune to be first danced by Grayson and Charlotte. Grayson stood up next to Charlotte at the table, presented his hand to her and said, "Mrs. Lee, would you kindly have this dance with me?"

"Why, but of course, Mr. Lee."

Grayson guided Charlotte out to the dance floor with his hand in hers held high out in front of him. They faced each other, and then he wrapped his other hand around her waist. He pulled her in close and then gazed into her eyes and whispered, "I love you." Charlotte repeated the words back to him.

When the song ended, Grayson waved to invite others to join. Slowly, a few couples came up until eventually the floor was packed. They sang and danced and enjoyed the evening celebration into the night.

***

"Am I the last one here?" Marty Denton had fallen asleep in his chair after one too many shots of whiskey. He was the town's drunk, but always friendly.

"Yes. We're all going to bed now, but Jarrod will take you home."

"Oh, I can get home myself." He got up, but then stumbled and fell back in the chair.

"No, I don't think so, Marty. Jarrod doesn't mind."

"Well alright, just this once."

"Right." Grayson, Jarrod and many others on numerous occasions had brought Marty home, but he never remembered.

"Thanks, Jarrod. I'll see you in the morning. Try to be quiet when you return."

"Won't you still be up with Charlotte?" Jarrod winked.

"That's none of your business. And besides that, Miss Jean will be sleeping here anyway."

"Yeah, yeah. I'll be quiet." Jarrod pushed Marty up into the back of the buckboard, threw a blanket over him and headed up the road over the hill.

***

Grayson put his arm around Charlotte and asked, "Ready for bed?"

"Yes. It's been a long day. I'm so tired."

"Uh. Yeah, I guess it has been a long day."

When they got upstairs in the bedroom, Charlotte changed into her nightgown, shyly facing away from Grayson in the dark corner of the room.

"Charlotte, you don't have to be modest with me. I'm your husband now."

"Yes, I know. I guess it's gonna take some getting used to."

Grayson got under the covers and then patted the other side of the mattress. "Come on to bed." Charlotte slowly got under the covers, staying close to the edge of her side of the bed.

"What are you doing way over there? Come over and give me a hug."

"Well…okay." Charlotte rolled over towards Grayson and felt his warm body touch hers. He wrapped his arm around her and gave her a light kiss on her lips and then her neck. "You're not tired?" Charlotte wasn't sure if she was ready to consummate the marriage tonight or not, but she knew by now that Grayson was.

"Not too tired to make love to you. I've waited so long. I don't think I can wait any longer, unless you tell me otherwise, of course."

Charlotte kissed him back. "I love you, Grayson."

"I love you too, Charlotte."

***

The next morning, Charlotte arose refreshed and energized after having a very good night's sleep. Grayson was tender, gentle and very loving with her during their first night together. She hadn't really known what to expect since she didn't have her mother or anyone else to ask about adult relationships and wedding nights, but it was better in some ways than she had expected, although somewhat uncomfortable too. She figured it would get better the more they were together in the years to come.

Charlotte and Grayson made their way downstairs and were greeted by Jarrod and Miss Jean already having breakfast.

"Well, good morning, Mr. and Mrs. Lee. Sleep well?" Jarrod asked with a smile and eyebrows raised.

"Yes," they replied in unison and then laughed.

"Good. Join us for breakfast." Miss Jean put two plates down on the table.

"Thanks, Miss Jean." Grayson smiled and squeezed the back of Miss Jean's shoulders with his hands.

"Yes, thank you Miss Jean. Is Jenni up yet?" Charlotte asked.

"She was up earlier, and I fed her, but now she's taking a nap."

"Thank you. I know that's my responsibility now. I don't usually sleep in like this."

"I'll give you some leeway since it was your wedding night and all." Miss Jean peered through the top of her eyeglasses like a scolding school teacher. "I don't expect either of you to make it a habit though."

"Of course not, Miss Jean. You know me. I'm always up early." Grayson grabbed another biscuit and more bacon for his plate.

"And I'll be up to cook your breakfast, dear." Charlotte stroked Grayson's back.

"Married life is good." Grayson looked up at Charlotte with a big smile.

"It always is the first morning," Jarrod said.

"Just wait and see when the right girl comes around and knocks you off your feet," Grayson replied.

"Yeah, I've been waiting and no one has so far."

"You'll see." Grayson pointed at Jarrod with his fork. "And then *I* can tease YOU."

"Unless I'm too old to hear you by then." Jarrod cupped his ears.

"Don't be such a pessimist. You'll find someone sooner than that. You just can't be so fussy."

"I'll be as fussy as I want to be." Jarrod's voice got louder and his eyes widened. "Especially if I have to spend the rest of my life with her."

"Alright, calm down now. It's your life, I guess. Would be nice if you still have your teeth though when you meet her." Grayson chuckled.

"Ha. Ha. Ha. Why don't you just be quiet and finish your breakfast?"

"Now that's enough from you two already. And yes, finish your breakfast so you can get to cleaning up the mess left outside from last night." Miss Jean got up from the table and gathered the dishes to the sink.

"Yes, Miss Jean," Grayson and Jarrod said in unison.

Charlotte looked over at Miss Jean. "Please leave those dishes in the sink, Miss Jean. I'll wash them directly after I've finished eating. You already made us breakfast and all. Why don't you relax and have a seat on the porch for awhile? When I'm done with the dishes, I'll make us some tea and join you."

"You did marry the right girl, Grayson. That sounds lovely, Charlotte." Miss Jean went out the front door.

"Miss Jean likes you." Grayson smiled and put his hand on Charlotte's shoulder.

"I hope so. And I want you to like me too, Jarrod."

"Oh, I do Charlotte. I'm glad to see Grayson has found someone like you. Don't take it the wrong way when I tease Grayson. We do it to each other all the time."

"I think I'm starting to realize that."

"Well I'll get started on the mess outside. I'll see you out there, brother."

"Yeah, I'll be joining you soon."

Jarrod grabbed the last biscuit and walked out the door. Charlotte got up from the table, gathered the rest of the dishes and began washing them. Grayson came up behind her, gave her a big hug and a kiss on the cheek. "I'll be outside with Jarrod. Then we have some ranch work to do. I'll be back around lunch time. You'll have the rest of the morning to spend with Jenni and get to know her better."

"Yes. I'll finish these dishes and tidy things up and clean up whatever's left outside. And yes, Jenni and I will have some nice time together."

Grayson put on his hat and opened the front door, then looked back at Charlotte. "I love you."

"I love you too."

CHAPTER EIGHT

Over a month had passed and Charlotte was getting used to married life as well as adjusting to western life. The girl from the city was now milking cows and churning butter, something she never saw herself doing while living in Boston only a few months ago. But she was starting to not only tolerate this simple hard-working lifestyle, but actually beginning to embrace and enjoy it. And every day that passed, she fell more in love with Grayson as did he with her. Everything was perfect. So she thought.

Charlotte also loved being a mom to Jenni and was looking forward to having a baby with Grayson soon. Lately, she was feeling kind of queasy in the mornings, but thought is was nothing. No one had ever told her about morning sickness or really anything about being in the family way. She thought if her symptoms continued or got worse, then she would make a visit to the doctor, but wouldn't tell Grayson or anyone until she knew what was wrong.

***

Several people waved to Charlotte as she walked down the town's dirt road. She hesitantly waved back.

Sid looked up from behind the hotel front desk and saw Charlotte approaching with a suitcase in hand. "Good afternoon, Miss Charlotte. Are you going somewhere?"

"No. I just arrived. I'm guessing you and everyone else in town are mistaking me for my twin sister, Cheryl."

"Cheryl? I don't know a Cheryl. But I do know Charlotte, and she looks just like you."

"Sounds like she's fooled everyone. Her name is Cheryl, and I assume she is with Grayson at his ranch. Can you be so kind as to tell me how to get there?"

"Huh? I'm confused. Charlotte or err, Cheryl never said she had a twin. I guess I didn't even know she had a sister for that matter."

"I'm not surprised she didn't tell you or anyone else."

"Yes, I reckon so. Um, well you can go to the ranch, if you can find someone to take you, but Grayson or his brother, Jarrod, usually comes into town about this time every week to get supplies and pick up the mail. If you wait around a bit, I'll bet one of them will show up."

"That sounds fine. In the meantime, I would like to get a room. Do you have one available?"

"Yes, I do. Just sign this and I'll get you your key and show you to your room. When I see Grayson or Jarrod I'll let them know you're here."

"Thank you." Charlotte went to her room, freshened up and changed her clothes and waited for either Grayson or Jarrod to arrive.

***

Sid saw Grayson pass by on his buckboard and went outside to tell him about Charlotte. "Hey, Grayson!"

"Well, hey there Sid. How are you?"

"Good. Um…There's someone in the hotel to see you."

"See me? Who?"

"I think you should just go meet her and find out for yourself."

"HER? A woman? Who is it, Sid?"

"She's in room two. She'll let you know who she is."

"Why you being all funny?"

"You'll see."

"Alright, well I don't have a lot of time to spare. I got stuff to take care of so enough of this mystery talk. Let me just go see who it is. Can you at least tell me her name?"

"Charlotte."

"Charlotte? Do you mean my Charlotte?"

"Not exactly."

Grayson shook his head and then put the brake on the wagon and went directly to room two and knocked on the door. As the door opened, Grayson began to speak, "Hello Ma'am. Sid told me..." He stopped mid-sentence as he raised his head. "Charlotte? What are you doing here?"

Charlotte opened the door wider and then rushed into Grayson and gave him a big hug. "Oh Grayson, it's so good to finally meet you!"

"Wait a minute. What's going on here? You sort of sound like Charlotte. You certainly look like Charlotte. But for some reason, I don't think you are Charlotte. Who are you?"

"But I am Charlotte. The one you have been writing to. It's my twin sister, Cheryl, that you are confusing me with."

"Cheryl? Twin sister? What?"

"I never told you about my twin sister. We never got along, and I barely consider her family. I just didn't see any reason to mention her in my letters to you."

"But she calls herself Charlotte. She arrived here acting as if she was you. For goodness sakes, we got married!"

"Married? Oh, I was hoping that hadn't happened yet."

"Well, it has. And I'm really confused now. I thought she was you. But now here you are standing in front of me telling me I married your sister! How did that happen?"

"She knew I was receiving letters from you, a handsome and wealthy man. I knew she was jealous, but I never knew she would stoop so low. She somehow intercepted your last few letters, but one more came after she left. The one where you said you were so happy that I agreed to marry you. I was shocked and confused. I found one of your previous letters in some of Cheryl's belongings that she left behind. And then it all made sense. We didn't know where Cheryl was going when she left. She just took off one day without much of an explanation, but then I put two and two together and realized what she did. I borrowed some money from my Aunt and got on a train as soon as I could. I was praying the entire way that you hadn't got married yet, but it looks like my prayers weren't answered."

"I don't know what to say. I'm completely dumbstruck."

"Even though you're married, it's not too late for us, Grayson. You can get an annulment and then WE can get married."

"Hold on. Just hold on. I need time to think."

"What's there to think about?"

"It's terrible to know that my marriage is based on a lie. And the woman I married lied to me. But I cannot help or deny the truth that I have fallen in love with your sister."

"But what about all the words we exchanged in our letters to each other? Doesn't that mean anything to you? Didn't you fall in love with ME through those letters?"

"Of course it meant something, and I WAS falling in love with you, but now everything has changed. I really don't know what to do. I don't know if I can forgive Cheryl."

"Forgive Cheryl? You don't have to forgive Cheryl. Just have the marriage annulled and marry me."

"But I do love your sister. At least I think I do." Grayson furrowed his brow, looked away from Charlotte and rubbed his head.

"Don't you love me?"

"I don't know anymore. I thought Cheryl was you. And now she's not, but you're here now, and I'm so confused."

"Well at the very least, you can give me a chance. We need to spend some time together and talk, since we never have until now."

"But how does that look? I'm married, but I'm gonna get to know you like we're courting?"

"Let me spend the week with you, and then you can decide who you want."

"And Cheryl is just gonna step aside while I get to know you?"

"I'll take care of Cheryl. It's the least she can do. I'm giving her a fair chance, even though she didn't do the same for me. She stole you from me!"

"I reckon she did."

"One week, then you decide. Fair enough?"

"Fair enough, I guess."

"Good. I'll stay at your ranch, in a separate bedroom of course, and Cheryl will stay at the hotel for the week."

"This is going to be awfully confusing to Jenni. She's just starting to warm up to Charl...I mean Cheryl. How am I going to explain all this to her? She already calls her mommy."

"Yes, I don't want to cause any more strife for Jenni than need be. She's just a child. But I need to have time with Jenni as well and can't have Cheryl there in the house at the same time. We will tell Jenni that Cheryl had to stay in town for a short time, but will be back."

"Will she?"

"I guess that will be up to you."

"This is just crazy. I thought everything was right again for me. I got married, have a lovely wife and new mother to my child and now everything is turned upside down."

"I don't want to cause you pain, Grayson. But I cannot leave without giving us a chance. I would regret it for the rest of my life. Wouldn't you?"

"In some ways, I wish you never came. But I guess now that you're here, I need to know too. Gosh, darn it. I just want to live a simple life."

"A week and then you can return to your simple life with the right woman."

"I hope it's that simple."

"I hope and pray it is too."

CHAPTER NINE

Grayson walked through the front door of the cabin where he found Charlotte, who was actually Cheryl, cooking dinner.

"You're home early. Did you get all the supplies you needed in town?"

"No." Grayson took off his hat, placed it on the rack and then stared at the back of Cheryl as she cooked. "No, I didn't."

"Well, why not?"

"Because I ran into your sister."

Cheryl immediately stopped stirring and turned around to look at Grayson. "My sister?" What do you mean, MY SISTER?" She began to tremble and got an awful feeling in the pit of her stomach. She almost fainted, but then caught herself on the kitchen chair. Grayson ran over and helped her sit down.

"Charlotte, I guess I mean Cheryl—don't I?" Grayson pulled a chair up and sat down in front of Cheryl who was staring out the ground. He gently put his hand under her chin and lifted her head so he could see her eyes. "You need to tell me right here and now the whole truth about who you are and why you're here."

"But *I am* Charlotte! Cheryl is my twin sister. I knew she was jealous of me receiving those letters from you and your proposal for marriage, but I never thought she would come all the way out here and try to pretend she's me. That's just crazy."

"Are you telling me that she's the one that's lying and not you?"

"That's right. And why are you even questioning me? Don't you love me?" Cheryl's voice trembled as tears began to run down her cheeks.

"Well that's the problem. Of course I love you." Grayson stood up, pushed the chair aside and turned away. "But I got to know who's telling the truth."

"I am. I wouldn't lie to you." Cheryl walked over to Grayson and gently put her hand on the back of his shoulder.

"There is only one way to know for sure."

"What's that?"

"The woman in the hotel who claims she's you says that you stole the last few letters I sent to Charlotte. She did not get the letter where I proposed and just kept waiting for my letters to arrive."

"That's nonsense."

"I wrote one more letter that supposedly arrived after you left and that's how she figured what you did and why she's here now."

"I came out as soon as I received your proposal and the money for the train ticket from you. I didn't know you wrote another letter."

"Well, I did. And there's really only one way to know for sure if you're telling me the truth."

Cheryl looked up at Grayson and hesitated. "What's that?"

"Even if one of you intercepted a few letters, only the one who wrote to me knows what was said in those letters to me. Only she and I know."

"Yes…"

"So aside from the last letter that you wrote to me where you accepted my proposal, tell me something that you wrote to me that only you and I would know. I've kept all your letters. I almost know everything you've written to me by heart since I would read them several times over."

"Well, let me think." Cheryl placed her finger on her lip and stared at the floor.

"Anything, Charlotte." Grayson turned her around to face him."ANYTHING."

"Oh, I'm getting all rattled. You're putting a lot of pressure on me. I'm having a hard time remembering right now. Those letters are from awhile back."

Grayson released her from his grip and stepped back. "You're starting to make me nervous, Charlotte. Or should I call you Cheryl?"

More tears started to stream down her face. She put her head in her hands and began to cry out loud. "I'm so sorry, Grayson. I didn't think she would find out."

"Find out what?"

"That I stole her letters. I figured when she stopped receiving letters from you that she would think you weren't interested anymore. I didn't know your wrote one more letter. I thought she would just forget about you and move on. I never thought she would come out here and find us."

"You're Cheryl?"

"Yes, I'm Cheryl, Charlotte's twin sister. Did she ever mention me to you in her letters?"

"No."

"I just thought I would come out here and find this great man that she talked about and marry him, and I would be taken care of. I knew I would like you. I didn't know if I would or could love you. But to my surprise, I have fallen in love with you. Deeply in love, Grayson."

Grayson was shocked at Cheryl's words. "But you lied to me. I thought you were someone else. I thought you were Charlotte. I don't know who *Cheryl* is."

"But you do know me. I haven't pretended to be anyone else. I was afraid something that you and Charlotte discussed in a letter may come up, but it never did. I guess not until now. I have just been myself, and I thought you liked me for who I am. I thought you'd fallen in love with me too."

"I did fall in love with you. But I cannot ignore the fact that you lied to me. Everything that I thought I knew was happening between you and I was based on a lie. I cannot forget that."

"But can you forgive?"

"I don't know, Cheryl. And now Charlotte wants me to spend time with her for one week and then choose between the two of you."

"What! But I am your wife. You're married to me. She has come too late. You cannot do such a thing."

"It sounded crazy to me too. But I fell in love first with the woman in the letters. The woman named Charlotte."

"But what about me?"

"I don't know anymore. I'm so confused. But I think I owe it to Charlotte and myself to at least get to know the woman my marriage proposal was meant for."

"And what if I say I don't agree with this?"

"You can disagree. I understand that much. But what about me? Can't you see where I'm coming from? The woman I thought I married is actually someone else. And the one I was supposed to marry, I've barely even spoken to. I've got to know who she is."

"And what happens after the week is over?"

"I'll decide what's best for me and Jenni."

"I really have no say in this?"

"Under the circumstances, no."

"Just know that I love you with all my heart. I love Jenni too. And know that I'm sorry for what I've done. I didn't want to hurt you. That was never my intention."

"I know. Well, I guess I think I know, but at this moment, I really don't know what to think."

"Can I at least give you a hug?" Charlotte walked towards Grayson, but he stepped back, refusing her approach.

"No. I think I just want to be alone now. I need you to pack a bag so you can stay at the hotel for the week."

"And she's going to stay where?"

"Here. In a room by herself. I can't be riding back and forth to town everyday to spend time with her."

"This is just preposterous." Cheryl placed her hands on her hips. "I'm your wife and you're going to have another woman in the house while I stay in a hotel?"

"I don't see any other way. Please don't argue with me anymore." Grayson put on his hat and went outside to the barn. Cheryl went upstairs, sat down on the edge of the bed and again began to cry.

***

Grayson took Cheryl to town later that evening and got her a hotel room.

"Which room is my sister in?"

Grayson whispered angrily, "You're not going to see your sister. Not at least until the end of the week. I don't want to see or hear any confrontation between the two of you. It will just make things even more complicated and difficult than they already are."

"Well, I never…"

"Not now you won't." Grayson carried her bag into the room, gave her some money for the week and went to close the door behind him, but Cheryl stopped him before it could close.

"Aren't you at least going to say goodnight?"

"Goodnight, Cheryl."

"That's it?"

"For now it has to be." Grayson walked away as Cheryl closed the door behind him, sat on the bed and began to cry again. Cheryl thought about knocking on the hotel room doors until she found her sister, but it was very late, and she didn't want to wake the wrong person up. She would listen in the morning when Grayson picked Charlotte up and confront her then.

***

Grayson did not want to give either Charlotte or Cheryl the chance to wake up early and find each other so he arrived at the hotel before dawn. He lightly knocked on Charlotte's door and whispered her name a few times before she finally cracked the door.

"Grayson?" Charlotte peered through the door crack with squinted, sleepy eyes. "Why are you here so early?"

"Get dressed so I can take you back to my ranch."

"Where's Cheryl? What did she say?"

"I'll tell you on the way back to the ranch."

Charlotte put on a dress, gathered her belongings and went down to the buggy with Grayson.

"The sun hasn't even risen yet. Are you always up this early?"

"Not always." Grayson grabbed the reins, and they headed out of town back to the ranch. On the way, he told Charlotte what Cheryl had said to him and that she agreed to a week.

"I'm surprised she agreed to that. I'm also surprised she admitted to lying."

"Well, she didn't exactly confess outright. I had to force it out of her. She had no choice when I asked her about the letters."

"I guess she feels guilty enough for what she did to give me and you this chance. Now it's my turn to get to know you. I feel like I already know a lot about you, but it's different being with you in person."

"This is all so weird to me. Like it's not really happening. Give me a day to adjust."

"I understand. I just want us to have a chance. After all those words we said to each other, I can't just walk away. Not like this. Not the way my sister manipulated both of us."

"But I do have feelings for your sister. Yesterday, before you came, I was undoubtedly in love with her."

"And today?"

"Confused."

"Well, I hope by the end of this week you won't be confused anymore."

"God willing."

***

Jarrod and Miss Jean were on the porch when Grayson and Charlotte arrived. They did not know about Cheryl yet.

"Jarrod, Miss Jean. This is Charlotte."

"Yeah, we know who Charlotte is. Did you forget?" Jarrod chuckled.

"It's a long story, but this is Charlotte Chadwick, Cheryl's twin sister."

"Who's Cheryl?" Miss Jean asked.

"Cheryl is the one I married. Charlotte is the one I had been writing to. There's been a mix-up of sorts."

"Mix-up? What?" Jarrod scratched his head.

Charlotte extended her arm to greet Miss Jean. "Pleasure to meet you, Ma'am."

"Why you look just like Charlotte, but you speak a little differently." Miss Jean slowly put out her hand to shake Charlotte's.

"Yes, Cheryl is my identical twin. Nice to meet you, Jarrod."

"Well, I'll be." Jarrod took off his hat and lightly cupped his hand under Charlotte's. "Pleasure, Ma'am. Boy, you would have fooled me!"

Grayson took Charlotte inside and showed her to her room. He then went outside to talk to Jarrod and Miss Jean on the porch.

"What in the world is going on, brother?"

"Charlotte has a twin sister, Cheryl. The woman who I thought was Charlotte and married was actually Cheryl. She stole my last letters to Charlotte and pretended to be her so that I would marry her. Charlotte didn't even know that I proposed. She thought I stopped writing and wasn't interested in her. But one letter came after Cheryl left. And now she's here."

"And she knows you've already married Cheryl?" Miss Jean asked.

"Yes."

"So why is she here at the ranch? And where's Cheryl?"

Grayson further explained to Miss Jean and Jarrod about Charlotte staying the week so they could get to know each other.

"Well, aren't you in a mess." Jarrod consoled Grayson with a pat on his shoulder. "Women. I told you you're better off without them. They just cause trouble."

"I feel like I'm stuck in some horrible nightmare. I don't even know if what I'm doing is the right thing to do. I thought I loved Cheryl, but I also thought she was Charlotte. Any advice, Miss Jean?"

"Don't you want my advice?" Jarrod asked.

"Thanks, but no thanks."

"Well, fine. I'll let you figure it out. And I'm sure Miss Jean has some sensible words for you. I'll see you later. Good luck, brother."

"Yep. See you later." Jarrod walked off the porch and headed towards the coral. "So Miss Jean, what should I do?"

"You love Charl…I mean Cheryl, right?"

"Yes."

"If Charlotte came knocking at your door a year from now instead of yesterday, would you be doing the same thing as you are now? Would you have put Cheryl aside for a week to try out Charlotte?"

"Try out? That's a strange way of putting it. But, no. Probably not. Too much time would have passed."

"What's too much time?"

"I don't know. A few months."

"And what happens at the end of the week? Is that enough time for you to decide between the two of them?"

"It should give me some idea."

"Some idea isn't enough. You married Cheryl, for better or for worse, not for maybe until her sister comes around."

"But she lied to me. Our marriage was based on false pretenses."

"That is true. She has sinned and will have to settle that with God. And she will have to ask for your forgiveness. But can you forgive her?"

"I don't know."

"Well, that is what you have to figure out, not whether you like Charlotte better than Cheryl. You made a commitment to Cheryl, not Charlotte. The question is, do you love Cheryl and if so, can you forgive her?"

"I don't know."

"Well, you need to figure it out. You can't play with these girls' hearts. It's unfair to them. It's like you're trying out a horse to see if it is better and can replace the one you already have. Would you even consider trying out a new horse to replace Buck?"

"No, of course not."

"Exactly."

Grayson was now confused more than ever. Miss Jean was right. What he was doing was wrong. It wasn't fair to anyone.

Charlotte was the one he wrote to and liked enough to want to marry, but Cheryl was the one he fell in love with. He knew it was possible to love more than one woman in a lifetime. He had loved Laura, his wife and first true love. But then he fell in love with Cheryl. It didn't mean he wouldn't have fallen in love with Charlotte; he likely would have since she had many of the same characteristics, both inside and out as Cheryl. But likewise, he could probably say that of any other woman he might have met while single during his lifetime. Miss Jean was right. He said "I do" to Cheryl, not Charlotte.

CHAPTER TEN

Charlotte came out onto the porch where Grayson was sitting alone.

"It's very lovely here. So peaceful. And the air is so fresh. It's very different from the city."

"Yes. I love living here. It was where I was raised. Where I learned everything from my parents, and why I am the man I am today."

"I would have liked to have met your parents."

"Yes. They were good parents to me and my brother. They taught us all the important stuff in life, like working hard, being kind to your neighbors and living righteously."

"I wish both our parents were still alive."

"Yeah. I am grateful though for Miss Jean. She is like family to me. And she gives me good advice like an elder would, which reminds me... I thought I was doing the right thing by bringing you here and leaving Cheryl in town, but it isn't. Cheryl is my wife. I gave her my word in my vows to her as a husband to be there for her forever, no matter what."

"But you thought she was me. She lied to you. Doesn't that matter?"

"Of course it does. But she is still my wife, and you are not. I've been living with her for over a month now. We have been intimate, you know. Doesn't that matter to you?'

"Well, I didn't want to ask. I actually didn't want to know. It would be something I would have to overlook. It wouldn't stop me from marrying you, though."

"That's beside the point. I cannot abandon Cheryl, especially not after a week's time."

"Well, I can stay longer if you need more time. She will just have to accept it."

"No. That's not what I mean. It is very possible that I may find that I like you very much by the end of this week. That doesn't change what I already have with Cheryl. It's just not fair to you, Cheryl or myself, not to mention Jenni."

"What are you saying? Do you not want me? You haven't even given us a chance."

"I've come to the conclusion that no chance should be given. It's just not right. It's not that I don't like you. To tell you the truth, I really don't know what I feel right now."

"Will you stay with Cheryl then?"

"That's something I have to figure out."

"And if you don't stay with Cheryl, then what?"

"I will be alone again."

"So what I am supposed to do? Just turn around and leave? I just traveled for weeks on a train and then a long, uncomfortable stagecoach ride to see you. I'm not getting back on that stage or train. At least not anytime soon."

"Well, I can't have you stay here. I guess the least I can do is put you up at the hotel. This way you can talk to your sister and perhaps resolve your relationship with her. That's your family. That's your blood kin. No matter what, you should always try to have a good relationship with your kin. Family should always have each other's back because in the end, sometimes that's all you got."

"Yes, but kin shouldn't hurt you and that's exactly what Cheryl did to me."

"No, they shouldn't. But sometimes people make mistakes. You need to think about forgiving her."

"Like you should?"

"I reckon. But I don't want to talk about that with you. I need to get Cheryl back here. Please gather your things, and I'll take you back to town."

"I don't like this one bit, Grayson. But if you really don't want to get to know me, I guess I can't force you."

"It's not that, Charlotte. I don't want to explain it again. Can't you understand?"

"Perhaps in time, but not right now." Charlotte walked away and went back into the cabin and packed her things. She came out back to the porch with her bag in hand and tears rolling down her cheeks. "If I have to go, then let's go."

Grayson saw her tears and the distraught look on her face. "Oh, Charlotte. I'm sorry for all this. I'm sorry for what Cheryl has done to you…and me."

"Let's just go." Charlotte walked over to the buggy. Grayson took her bag and helped her up. They didn't speak a word to each other the entire way back to town.

***

Grayson helped Charlotte to her room. "Cheryl is in room five. I'll let you two spend some time together to talk things through and then return for her in the morning."

Charlotte replied coldly, "Thank you. I'll take care of things from here."

"I'm sorry Charlotte. I…"

"No need to say anything more, Grayson. I'm sorry too. I'm sorry I came. I'm also sorry I ever replied to your ad."

"You don't mean that Charlotte, do you?" Grayson reached out to touch her arm, but she pulled away.

"After all this time and emotions invested in a man, and what do I get in return? Nothing. I wanted a husband, and all I got is a train ride back to Boston."

"I don't know what to say anymore."

"Then don't say anything and please leave."

Grayson closed the door behind him and returned to the ranch. He didn't want to be present when the two sisters met again.

Charlotte immediately proceeded to room five and knocked on the door. Cheryl opened it quickly, hoping it was Grayson. "Gray…Oh, Charlotte. I wasn't expecting to see you."

"Let me in your room so we can talk. I don't want the entire hotel hear us speak."

Cheryl opened the door wide, and Charlotte quickly walked in and turned around with arms crossed. She spoke angrily, but controlled the volume so others would not hear. "How could you do this to me? How could you steal Grayson away from me?"

"I didn't steal him away from you. I came out here, and he chose to marry me."

"But he thought you were me!"

"But he got to know me and fell in love with me, NOT YOU. So does it really matter who he thought I was?"

"Of course it does. It matters to me, and it matters to him."

"Well, I thought that's why I'm giving you two a week to decide."

"He doesn't want to do that anymore. He doesn't want to get to know me."

"What? Why? Does he not want me either?"

"He's trying to decide on that. Apparently he thinks his word in marriage to you is more important than anything else. But he's still not sure he can forgive you."

"So where is he? Did he bring you back here?"

"Yes. He said he would come back tomorrow to pick you up. He wanted us to talk because we are sisters, and we shouldn't be estranged from each other, since we're family and all."

"I guess he's right about that." Cheryl sat down on the edge of the bed.

"Well, you have no reason to be mad at me. I'm the one who is hurt and betrayed."

"I know what I did was wrong. I just wanted a different life than what we had. We both were answering mail-order bride ads, and you were the lucky one to have someone like Grayson reply to you. At first I was just jealous. But then I was starting to feel desperate. Time was slipping away, and I felt if I waited too long, no man would want me. I shouldn't have stolen those letters, but once I did I felt Grayson was mine to have."

"And how am I supposed to forgive you for that?"

"I don't know, Charlotte. But I do know I want you to be in my life. I at least want to know I have a sister who doesn't hate me." Cheryl got up from the bed and tried to put her hand on Charlotte's shoulder, but Charlotte brushed her away.

"And what if Grayson doesn't forgive you?"

"I'll be devastated. But even more so if I don't have my sister by my side either. I know we haven't gotten along in the past, but I really want things to change between us."

"I'm starting to understand how Grayson must feel. I'm just as confused. I'm even more hurt. I cannot talk to you anymore right now."

"I understand. I'll be here if you want to talk later."

"Grayson has been kind enough to put me up in this hotel for the week. I suppose I will see you during this time, and perhaps we can talk again."

"Okay, Charlotte."

Charlotte walked out the door and went back to her room. She stayed in there until the next morning when she heard a knock on her door.

***

Charlotte opened the door surprised to see Jarrod standing there. She thought it would be Cheryl, or maybe even Grayson. "Why, hello Jarrod."

"Morning, Miss Charlotte." Jarrod removed his hat, pressing it to his chest.

"What are you doing here?"

"Well, Grayson picked Cheryl up earlier this morning and took her back to the ranch. Grayson felt bad you wouldn't have anyone in town to talk to for awhile so he asked if I would come in and see if you would have breakfast with me."

"I don't need anyone to pity me. I'm fine, thank you."

"Oh, I didn't mean it to sound like that. When I met you yesterday, even though it was brief, I thought you seemed like a real nice gal. I had to come into town anyway to pick up some things. Even if Grayson hadn't asked me, I still would have stopped by and said hello."

"That's kind of you Jarrod. You've said hello, but do you really have the time or even want to have breakfast with me?"

"I do. I honestly do. Miss Jean fixed me something at the ranch this morning, but it don't matter 'cause I'm pretty much always hungry. And the food here at the hotel is pretty tasty."

"Well, I guess you've convinced me. Let me just fix my makeup and I'll be down right away."

"Makeup? You don't need to fix anything. You look beautiful just the way you are."

"You really must be hungry."

"Well, yes. I am. But I mean what I say. You are pretty."

"And flattery will get you everywhere, including to the breakfast table." Charlotte smirked. "Shall we?"

"Yes, Ma'am." Jarrod presented his arm, which Charlotte accepted. He walked her down the stairs into the dining room and pulled out the chair for her.

"I didn't think you wild western men would have such nice manners."

Jarrod removed his hat and sat down after Charlotte. "Why, yes, Ma'am. Grayson and I and most men out here always treat women with the greatest respect, even if we don't like 'em. It's how we were raised."

Charlotte laughed. "Well, I hope you like me."

"Yes, Ma'am."

"Please call me Charlotte."

"Yes, Miss Charlotte."

"Just Charlotte is fine."

"Okay, Ma'…I mean Charlotte."

Charlotte and Jarrod ate their breakfast, but then spent at least another hour talking to each other. They found they enjoyed each other's company. Jarrod was not Grayson, but he had a charming way about him that Charlotte really liked. And he did have the same good looks as his brother: tall and muscular, chestnut wavy hair, dark brown eyes and a strong chiseled face. Charlotte was certainly still heart-broken about Grayson, but was enjoying this distraction.

Jarrod was surprised he enjoyed talking to Charlotte and being with her. He really never talked to women, except for a few minutes of chit-chat every now and then. He was close to being married before, but he found out she had cheated on him and vowed never to be involved with another woman again. She had broken his heart and he didn't want to feel that much pain and vulnerability again. Over the last couple years, he had been content being alone and doing his own thing: working the ranch when he wanted to, hunting when he wanted to, going to the saloon when he wanted to. He had no interest in getting to know another woman. At least not until now.

"Gosh, the time has flown by. I got to get going." Jarrod wiped his face and then threw down the napkin on the table.

"Well, thank you for breakfast. I had a nice time talking to you."

"Me too, Charlotte. I haven't talked this long to a woman in years."

"Will you be in town again before I leave?"

"I hadn't planned on it, but it would nice to see you again. I could meet you the day after tomorrow, and we could have dinner. I would say sooner, but I there's some things I need to take care of on the ranch."

"Yes, that would be nice. I'm only staying here to work things out with my sister before I leave, but it sure would be nice to have someone else to spend time with before I go."

Jarrod got up from the table and then pulled out Charlotte's chair and extended his hand to help her up. "I'll see you Thursday for dinner then."

"Yes. I look forward to it."

Charlotte went back to her room with mixed feelings. Just yesterday, she had lost her would-be husband that she thought would be the love of her life to her sister who had betrayed her. And this morning, through one long conversation and meal with her ex-beau's brother, she experienced a feeling of connection, perhaps even romance.

After getting his supplies, Jarrod rode back to the ranch, and all he could think about was Charlotte. In some ways he didn't want to have any thoughts. He even tried to think of other things, but Charlotte's beautiful face kept returning to his mind's eye. He thought to himself, IS THIS EVEN RIGHT? THIS WAS MY BROTHER'S GIRL. WHAT WOULD HE THINK? Before Jarrod would have dinner with Charlotte, he would have to talk to Grayson about it. He wanted to know it was okay. Family always came first.

CHAPTER ELEVEN

Jarrod walked through the door to find Grayson, Cheryl and Miss Jean having lunch.

Grayson wiped his mouth and looked up at Jarrod. "Well, you've been gone for quite some time. I know you had breakfast with Charlotte, but it shouldn't have taken that long. Did you have trouble getting supplies or something?"

"Naw. I didn't have any trouble." Jarrod didn't want to tell everyone that he had spent all that time with Charlotte. He wanted to talk to Grayson in private later. "I sure could eat though."

"Have a seat. We're just finishing up." Grayson rose from the table and carried his dishes to the wash basin. "I'll be back around supper time. I want to check on the herd and make sure those coyotes aren't back. Then I'm gonna check on the diversion ditch. The water's not flowing like it should."

"Want any help?" Jarrod asked with a full mouth of food.

"Naw, I'm good. I can handle it myself."

Grayson had talked to Cheryl some after he picked her up from the hotel on the way back to the ranch, but any issues between them were far from being resolved. He just wanted to do some ranch work to keep his mind busy with thoughts other than his marriage. He grabbed his hat and headed out the door.

Both Miss Jean and Cheryl sensed Grayson's anxiety and thought it was best to not say a word and let him be. Cheryl knew she had to win back his heart and, more importantly, his trust. For now, she would be silent and let him be. All she wanted to do was to give him a big hug and kiss, but knew he wouldn't be receptive to it right now. She hoped to begin convincing him later that evening.

Miss Jean pushed what was left of the stew and the last three rolls over to Jarrod. "Do you think this will be enough to fill that endless pit of a belly of yours, or at least to keep you from starving until dinner?"

"Yes, Ma'am. I think it'll do."

Cheryl and Miss Jean cleared off the remaining dishes from the table and washed and dried them. Miss Jean turned back to Jarrod, who was still eating. "Do you think you can do us the courtesy of washing your dishes all by yourself?"

"Yes, Ma'am."

"Thank you kindly. Now I think I'm going to take a rest out on the porch. I could use some fresh air."

"I'll get Jenni, and we'll come outside and join you," Cheryl said. Jenni was playing with her doll in the next room. "Come on, Jenni. We're gonna go outside with Miss Jean."

Jenni played while Miss Jean and Cheryl sat on the porch. For a good five or ten minutes, neither woman spoke a word. Cheryl knew that Miss Jean was angry with her. And Miss Jean was. Finally, the silence was broken. "Let me ask you one question."

"Yes, Ma'am?"

"Do you love Grayson with all your heart?"

"Yes, I do. I love Grayson and Jenni more than anything. I know what I did was wrong. My initial intentions did not come from a good place, but after getting to know Grayson and Jenni, things changed. It wouldn't have mattered to me whether he was rich or poor. I still would have married him."

"A man can't be with a woman he can't trust."

"I know, and I would never lie to him again. Aside from pretending to be Charlotte, I never have lied to him about anything else since we've been together. I would never deceive him again. I love him and just want to be his wife and a mother to Jenni."

"Well, I do believe in the sanctity of marriage, for better or for worse. This would definitely fall under worse. I do hope Grayson can find it in his heart to forgive you."

"I do too. I don't know what I'll do if he doesn't."

"Just pray and ask for forgiveness. That's all you can do."

"Yes, Miss Jean. I will. Every moment that passes."

Cheryl sat there with Miss Jean for a few more minutes and then suddenly felt very ill. She ran inside and vomited several times. Then she returned to the porch.

"I was gonna come check on you. What's wrong? Somethin' not agreeing with you?"

"I don't know. Lately I've been feeling kind of queasy and really tired. I've been having headaches and even my back hurts. I thought that was from churning butter, but I don't know why I've been feeling so awful lately. I was gonna go to see the doctor if it got worse."

"By gosh, are you in the family way?"

"Family way? I don't know. I've never been before."

"Well, of course not, but haven't you been around someone who has?"

"No Ma'am. Not that I know of."

"We need to get you to the doctor today. Come on. I'll take you. No need to bother Grayson with this."

"Yes, Ma'am." Miss Jean rode Cheryl into town with Jenni to see Doctor Turner. Cheryl was scared to think about being with child, especially with all this strife between her, Charlotte and Grayson. Miss Jean was silent on the ride in, only thinking to herself, shaking her head back and forth every few minutes and praying.

***

Jarrod met up with Grayson out near the creek where he was cleaning out the diversion ditch that sent water to the trough.

"How's it going?"

"It's flowing much better now that I got all that debris from the storm out."

"Good." Jarrod paused. He was somewhat hesitant to talk with Grayson about Charlotte, but he knew he had to.

"I think I'm pretty much finished here. Did you come out to help?"

"Well, yes. If you needed it. But I also wanted to talk to you."

"About what? I don't really want to talk to anyone right now about Cheryl. I got some thinking to do on my own about that. I've heard yours and Miss Jean's words about it. Now I got to figure it out for myself."

"Naw, I'm not gonna say another word about Cheryl to you. I...I want to tell you something about Charlotte."

"I really don't need to hear anything about Charlotte either, at least not anything to do with me and her being together."

"No, it's not that."

"Well, then what is it? I supposed you talked to her at breakfast. I'm glad you did that for her. But I don't need to know what she said."

"No. Just listen for a second. I just wanted to know if it was alright if I met with her for dinner."

"Dinner? That's nice of you to have another meal with her. Sure. Why not? Why are you asking me?"

"Well, I was checking to make sure. I know we always said we wouldn't court a girl that either of us had been with before."

"Court? I thought you were just having a meal with her to keep her company. Are you serious?"

"Well, no. I'm not sure. I don't exactly want to court her. But she's different than most of the women around here. I really liked spending time with her this morning."

"Oh, that's why you were so late. I would have never guessed, MR. I'M-NEVER-GETTING-MARRIED."

"No one said anything about getting married. I just want to spend some time with her while she's here, that's all."

"I have enough on my mind to worry about besides you and Charlotte. So I reckon I won't. Go ahead. Spend time with her. It is kind of weird for me. But if my brother is actually interested in a woman, even if it's Charlotte, then I won't stop you. You need someone to take care of you besides me and Miss Jean."

"You and Miss Jean don't take care of me. I'm fine just by myself."

"Never mind. But don't get your hopes up. She plans on leaving by the end of the week."

"Yeah. I know. But if things turn out right, maybe I could change her mind."

"And then what?" Grayson throws up his arms. "We'll all live here on the ranch, happily every after?"

"A man can dream, can't he?"

"Boy, you must be in love." Grayson knocked on Jarrod's head with his fist. "Who are you and what have you done with my brother Jarrod?"

"Quit it." Jarrod pushed Grayson away and got back on his horse. "You'll see."

"See what?"

Jarrod didn't reply. He smiled at Grayson and then galloped away.

Grayson wasn't really sure how he felt about his brother and Charlotte being together. He wanted to give Charlotte the week to spend some time with her sister to patch things up, knowing she would be gone after that. But how would he feel to have her around longer or even potentially have her as a sister-in-law? He wasn't even sure how he felt about Cheryl. He certainly had some praying to do as well as having some longer talks with his wife.

CHAPTER TWELVE

"Where's Jarrod? He's always on time for supper," Cheryl asked.

"He had some things to take care of. He said he probably would be a little late and not to wait for him." Grayson replied without looking up from his dinner plate.

"What's he doing?"

"Stuff."

Cheryl could sense that Grayson wasn't in the mood for questions or any discussion. But she knew she had to talk to him sooner or later about her visit to the doctor. She was scared of what his reaction would be. He already was having doubts about their relationship and now this.

After they finished supper, Cheryl finally got up the courage to speak with him. "Grayson, I need to talk to you."

"Well, I reckon I'm gonna need to talk to you too. I can't live like this, wondering if I can trust you or not. I love you and I don't want to dishonor our vows, but I need to be sure this is right."

"I know. All I can say is that I AM a trustworthy person. Before all this between me and you, I never acted in such a way."

"I just don't know, Cheryl. I thought I knew who you were, but I really didn't. Me and Charlotte wrote to each other for months and got to know each other that way. I only received one letter from you and really only knew you for less than a week before we got married."

"But we've been together now for nearly a couple of months. Don't you think you know me by now?"

"Well, I thought so, until Charlotte came to town."

"Yes, Charlotte. Do you still have any feelings for her?"

"No. Not really. Well, maybe some, but I decided to block her out of my mind since this problem is between me and you now, not her."

"The reason I wanted to talk to you is not about Charlotte or what I've done."

"What else could it possibly be? What else could be more important right now?"

"Grayson," Cheryl's voice quivered. "Grayson, we're going to have a baby."

"What? Are you sure?"

"Yes. Miss Jean took me to Doctor Turner this afternoon and confirmed it."

"A baby? Our baby?" Shocked, Grayson dropped his fork and leaned back in his chair.

"Yes."

Grayson was silent and then realized this was a joyful moment. His wife was carrying his unborn child. This changed everything about how he felt towards Cheryl. She was his wife, for better or for worse, and this was for better.

Grayson got up, walked over to Cheryl, took her hand and pulled her up from her chair and wrapped his arms around her. "I love you, Cheryl." Then he looked down and placed his hand on her lower abdomen. "And I will love our baby. He will have two loving parents and an older sister to look after him always."

"He?"

"He or she. It doesn't matter."

"Do you forgive me?"

"Yes. I do. I don't know how soon I'll forget, but I will forgive. But your word must always be true with me, as will mine with you."

"Oh, Grayson, I will never do such a thing to you again. I just want to be with you and Jenni and our baby. I just want to grow old with you and watch our children and grandchildren grow up. I just want to love you and our children and be a family together."

"Then that is what it will be, God willing."

Grayson and Cheryl hugged again and then called Miss Jean down from her room to tell her the news. She knew about Cheryl being with child, but was worried about Grayson and what his decision would be.

"Miss Jean?" Grayson called up the stairs. "Miss Jean?" The sound of a door being quickly shut and then opened again could be heard from upstairs.

"Yes?"

"Can you come down for a moment, please?"

"Yes. I'll be right there." Miss Jean slowly made her way down the stairs until she got to the last step.

"Miss Jean, me and Cheryl…"

Miss Jean cut Grayson's words off and replied, "Congratulations. I heard the whole thing from upstairs. Thin walls, you know."

"Why your hearing is better than I thought, especially behind a closed door and all." Grayson smirked.

"You know, somehow my door was cracked open. I need you to check the latch."

"Uh huh."

"Never mind that. I'm glad you two could resolve your problems, especially for Jenni and the baby's sake."

"Yes, we're glad too." Cheryl took Grayson's hand and squeezed it tight.

Just then, Jarrod came through the door. "What's going on? Everybody's smiling. Are those happy tears, Cheryl?"

"We're having a baby!"

"Baby? Well I'll be." Jarrod turned to Grayson. "I reckon by the looks of things, you and Cheryl will be staying together then?"

"That's right. 'Til death do us part."

"Good." Jarrod was happy for them, especially since he was becoming more interested in Charlotte.

Cheryl was relieved that Grayson forgave her and wanted to stay with her, but she also wanted Charlotte's forgiveness. She felt horrible about what she had done and didn't want her sister to leave on such bad terms. She decided she would go into town tomorrow morning and speak with her.

***

Jarrod walked confidently into the dining room, wearing his best shirt and vest and black ribbon neck tie. "Good evening, Miss Charlotte."

"Good evening, Jarrod. Why, how nice you look."

Jarrod looked down at himself and tugged on his vest. "Yep, I clean up real good. And you look as beautiful as always."

"Why, thank you."

"Have you ordered yet?"

"No. I just got here and wanted to wait until you arrived. I wasn't sure you would come."

"Not come? Nothing would have stopped me from coming. And besides that, if I tell you something or make a promise, I always make good on it. A man's word is everything."

"That's good to know. I've been disappointed many times before by men, present time included."

"Yeah, I'm sorry about what happened between you and my brother. You have to know that he feels bad about it and all. And things might have gone differently if you got here before he married Cheryl, and especially now that she's with child."

"With child?"

"Oops. That kind of slipped out. I reckon Cheryl should have been the one to tell you that."

"How long has she known?"

"Oh, not until just yesterday. She had been feeling ill for quite some time and didn't know why. Miss Jean took her to the doc's and he confirmed it."

"Well, that definitely changes everything." Charlotte looked down at the table in contemplation.

"Did you think you and Grayson would get back together?"

"No. Not really. In some ways I was hoping, but not after what he said the other day. I knew he was just going to decide whether or not to stay with Cheryl, not whether he would be with me."

"Well, he's definitely gonna stay with Cheryl now."

"I guess I should be happy for them, but it's hard for me to think that way right now. First I found out that she stole my fiancé, and now she's in the family way by him."

"I know it must be hard for you to be here. But I think Cheryl wants to make things right with you."

"I don't know if I can forgive her."

"She certainly has done you wrong. I can't argue with that. But she IS your sister. Grayson and I don't always get along, but I'm sure glad I have a brother that will always have my back."

"I suppose I can sit down and talk with her a few more times before I leave."

"In some ways, I hope you don't work things out with your sister by the end of the week."

"Why would you say that?"

"'Cause I'd like you to stay longer."

"Even if I do work things out with my sister by then, would you ask me to stay?"

"Maybe."

"Just maybe?"

"I can't lie, Charlotte. You intrigue me. And yes, maybe I'd like to get to know you better, if you would stay."

"What do you think Grayson would think about all this?"

"Oh, I already asked him and he said it was fine by him."

"Fine? I guess he really doesn't care about me anymore."

"It's not that, Charlotte. I'm sure he cares. Otherwise he wouldn't have asked me to see you or put you up for the week to make things right with your sister. If he really didn't care, he would have put you on the first stage out of here."

"I guess I need to move on then. And Jarrod, I do like you. You seem like a very kind man with a good heart."

Jarrod put his hand up to his mouth as if he was telling a secret and whispered across the table to Charlotte, "Don't tell any of the guys that, though."

Charlotte whispered back across the table, "No, of course not." She smiled and then continued speaking in her normal voice, "I can see you're also a very strong, confident man that can protect his woman and family if need be."

"That's right. That's me. I'm strong all right." Jarrod looked down at his bicep, made a fist and tightened his arm to somewhat subtly flex his muscles.

"Why, what big muscles you have," Charlotte said with a delicate, impressed voice.

"It's what many long days of hard ranch work will do to a man."

Jarrod and Charlotte enjoyed having another long meal together, just talking about their pasts, their likes and dislikes, never bringing up

Cheryl or Grayson in the conversation again. Charlotte was heartbroken over Grayson, but was enjoying her time with Jarrod. She wasn't falling in love. It was too quick for that. But she was enjoying the attention Jarrod was giving her and his company.

"Well, it's getting late and I need my beauty rest, you know."

"You couldn't possibly need any beauty rest. You're as beautiful as can be. Anything more would make you an angel."

"My, my, Jarrod Lee. You're quite the charmer, aren't you? How many times have you said line that to a woman?"

"Only once. Only when I meant it."

"So I'm the second?"

"The first and only." Jarrod took Charlotte's hand from across the table and gently placed a kiss upon it.

"Yes, quite the charmer. I shall say goodnight to you then. Thank you for dinner. I had a lovely time again with you."

Jarrod didn't want the night to end. "Hey, would you like to ride out just to the edge of town with me? It's a clear night, and I bet you don't have near as many stars to look at in that city of yours as we do here."

"Look at the stars?" Charlotte replied with a puzzled look.

"Yes."

"How novel. I've never really done such a thing."

"So now's your chance."

"Well alright. But will you protect me from all the night creatures you have out here?'

"You know I will." Jarrod flexed his muscles again, this time more boastfully.

"Okay, let's go, muscle man."

Jarrod drove the wagon out into the sagebrush, away from the noise of the town, where it was quiet and dark.

"Why, I've never seen so many stars before. Look at how they sparkle, like little diamonds. It is beautiful. Thank you for taking me out here, Jarrod. I would have never imagined it would've been so beautiful."

"Still not as beautiful as you."

"Now stop that already. You've made me blush so many times in the last few hours that I haven't any more blood left in my cheeks."

They both laughed. "I just want you to know that despite the reason you came out here, I'm glad you stayed and are with me at this very moment."

"Me too, Jarrod. Me too."

Jarrod placed a blanket from the back of the wagon around Charlotte. "Here, you look cold."

"Thank you." Charlotte was still sad about losing Grayson to Cheryl, but she knew she didn't have any chance with him anymore, especially now that Cheryl was expecting. She did like Jarrod, but what would that mean? Would she stay to get to know him better? How could she stay here and not only be in the same town with Grayson and Cheryl, but also with his brother? It was almost too much for her to think about.

"Can we go back now?"

"Oh sure. Are you getting too cold?"

"Yes, and tired. It's been a long couple days."

Jarrod took his jacket off and laid it across Charlotte's lap. "I'll get you back to the hotel in no time. This jacket might help keep the breeze off a little better."

"Thank you. And thank you again for the stars."

"I'd give you the stars and anything else you would like, Charlotte." Jarrod turned the wagon around and headed back into town. He helped Charlotte off and walked her back to her room.

"Will I see you again?"

"Of course. But I think you and Cheryl need to talk some more. She was going to come see you today, but she was feeling too ill. Grayson said she would come into town tomorrow to see you."

"Fine. Goodnight, Jarrod."

"Goodnight, Charlotte."

Charlotte tossed and turned, finding it hard to sleep. Her mind raced with thoughts about Cheryl, Grayson and Jarrod.

Jarrod, on the other hand, fell asleep quickly with sweet dreams about Charlotte as his wife.

CHAPTER THIRTEEN

Charlotte heard a knock on the door. She didn't expect it to be Jarrod, but was hoping it was. She opened the door, and to her disappointment, saw Cheryl standing there.

"Good morning, Charlotte."

"Morning, Cheryl."

"Can we talk?"

"Yes, I guess we must."

"Why don't we go downstairs and have breakfast together?"

"I suppose we could." Charlotte closed the door behind her, and they both walked down to the dining room.

Cheryl was nervous about talking with Charlotte, mostly about telling her that she was with child. She wasn't aware that Jarrod had already told Charlotte the night before. "How have you been?"

"I can't say this has been the happiest time of my life. I've been betrayed and worst of all, by my own sister."

"I know this was the worst thing I could have done. I was only thinking of myself when I took your letters and came out here to marry Grayson. I didn't even stop to think about how you would feel. To tell you the truth, I kind of blocked you out of my mind so I wouldn't feel bad about it. But since you've arrived, it's nearly all I've thought about. Oh, Charlotte, I'm so sorry. Could you every forgive me?" Cheryl put her head down and began to cry.

"Oh, stop that. Don't cause a scene. Perhaps one day I can forgive you, but it's not today. And I certainly will never forget what you've done. You have no idea how much you have hurt me, Cheryl."

"I'm so sorry. It's all I can say. I don't know what else to do."

"I think for now, you can leave. I'm still too upset to talk to you."

"Before I leave, I need to tell you something."

"If it's about you being in the family way, I already know. Jarrod slipped last night and told me during dinner."

"Oh." Cheryl looked down and paused. "And how do you feel about it?"

"I don't feel anything. I know though that you and Grayson must stay together now."

"Yes, we will."

"Good."

"I hate to leave you here all alone. I want to be able to talk to you again."

"Before the week's up, I'm sure we will. I'm just not in the mood right now. I'm too upset. But don't worry about me being alone. Jarrod has been nice enough to spend some time with me, and I appreciate it very much."

"Do you like Jarrod?"

"Why yes. I think he is a kind man."

"I think he likes you too."

"It would be nice to see him again before I leave."

"I don't think that will be a problem. He talks about you all the time."

"Good. I enjoy our conversations." Charlotte was curt with her answers, not wanting to let Cheryl know too much about her feelings about Jarrod, mostly because she wasn't sure herself.

"I will let him know."

"No, don't. If he wants to come see me, he can do so without being persuaded."

"Alright then. I will see you again sometime this week." Cheryl rose from the table and pushed her chair in. "Goodbye, Charlotte."

"Goodbye, Cheryl." Charlotte looked immediately down at her cup of coffee so Cheryl wouldn't have any more reason to speak.

Cheryl was somewhat relieved now that Charlotte knew about the baby and that she had no chance to be with Grayson anymore. She still hoped that they would work things out and that she and her sister would be on good terms before she left for Boston.

***

Jarrod rode into town the next day with the sole purpose of seeing Charlotte. As he pulled the buggy in front of the hotel, Charlotte happened to be walking out the door.

"Well, this is good timing."

"I was just stepping outside to get some fresh air. What are you doing here?"

"As if you didn't know. I've come to see you and take you back to the ranch."

"To the ranch? Aren't Cheryl and Grayson there?"

"Yes. But that doesn't matter, does it?"

"Perhaps it does. Why do you want to take me to the ranch?"

"I know Grayson brought you there already, but you didn't really get a chance to see much. I want you to see where I live and how I make my living. And besides that, it's a beautiful place. Much nicer than this dusty, old town. Aren't you getting tired of staring at those four walls in your room?"

"Why, yes, I am. But can't we go somewhere besides your ranch? I'm not sure I'm ready to see Grayson again. Especially not see the two of them together."

"It's not like we're going to spend time with them. It's a big ranch. We probably won't even see them. And they're certainly not going to be hugging on each other or anything like that, if that's what you're worried about. And besides, wouldn't you like to spend some time with me other than eating a meal?"

"Okay. You've convinced me. I'll go."

Jarrod was ecstatic that Charlotte agreed. He hopped out of the buggy, grinning ear to ear, and helped her up into the seat.

"Next stop, Wind River Ranch."

"I hope I don't regret this."

"Oh no you won't, Miss Charlotte. I guarantee it. When you're with me, only good things happen."

"Aren't you the confident one? I will never say you lack self-confidence."

"If you say so."

"I do." As they went down the road, they exchanged small talk, but nothing too serious. Charlotte was enjoying the scenery and Jarrod was simply enjoying her next to him. He wanted to impress Charlotte and make sure this afternoon was a pleasant experience for her. The week was almost over, and he wanted her to stay longer, but it would take some convincing. He had to make an offer she couldn't refuse.

***

Jarrod stopped the buggy in front of the barn.

"All of this is yours?" Charlotte was impressed by all the buildings and all the land Jarrod pointed out as theirs as they rode into the ranch. It had still been dark the previous morning when she rode in with Grayson and she wasn't able to see as much.

"Yes, Ma'am. Well, me and my brother's."

"Grayson mentioned a little bit about the ranch in his letters, but I had no idea is was this big."

"He's not one to brag. And he would have liked you to come because of him more so than because of the ranch."

"Of course. And I did. Well, I would have, that is."

"Here, let me show you around." Jarrod helped her out of the buggy, then showed her the barn and some of their farm animals and horses.

"I've always liked horses. I never rode one myself. In Boston, I see them mostly tied to the fancy carriages, pulling the wealthy folk around town."

"Would you like to ride one?"

"Yes. One day I'd like to give it a try."

"Why not now?"

"Oh, heavens no. I'm not appropriately dressed, and I would be afraid of falling off."

"Well, how about we both ride one together? I'll steer and keep things in control. You don't have to worry. I won't let you fall. We can take a ride down to the stream under the trees. It's a real pretty spot."

"I don't know, Jarrod…"

Before she could refuse, Jarrod saddled and bridled his horse. "This is Clover, my lucky charm."

Jarrod's gelding was born to the same mare and stallion as his brother's the following year. At first glance, it looked identical to Grayson's horse, Buck, but stood a little taller at exactly fifteen hands. Jarrod instantly wanted the colt so he could be just like his older brother. The horses looked so much alike, even their father was not able to tell which of the brothers were riding up to the house until they stopped to open the gate. The only difference was Jarrod's horse had a small white pattern on the right front foot that resembled a four-leaf clover. Jarrod felt he was lucky to have such a horse, and so named him Clover.

Jarrod patted the horse on the side of his neck. "I've had him since I was a young boy. I trust him with my life. He won't ever buck you off, especially since he knows how special you are."

"How does he know I'm special?"

"'Cause I told him so. C'mon. Here, let me help you up."

"Well, I insist on riding sidesaddle. I cannot sit astride in this dress."

"No problem." Jarrod then quickly lifted her up before she could object.

"Oh! I feel like I'm going to fall off!"

"Just hold onto that horn for a second while I get on." Jarrod hopped onto the horse, sitting just behind the cantle. He then reached around Charlotte to grab a hold of the reins. "There now. With my arms around you like this, you won't fall off. Feel better?"

"No. Not really."

Jarrod then gave Clover a firm kick and before Charlotte could scream, they were off in nearly a full gallop.

"Aaaahhh! Slow down, Jarrod! Slow down this second!"

Jarrod pulled up on the reins to slow down Clover to a trot and finally a much smoother walk. "Sorry. I just wanted to show you that you were safe. Now that we got that out of the way, you can enjoy the rest of the ride."

"Scaring me half to death is not an appropriate way to introduce me to horseback riding."

"But you feel safe now, don't you?"

"Safe would not be my first choice of words to describe how I'm feeling right now."

"Exhilarated?"

"I suppose that's closer."

"Good. I knew you would like it."

Charlotte was frightened at first, but maybe exhilarated WAS a good choice of words to describe how she was feeling. She was having a good time being with Jarrod and having her first ride on a horse in this most beautiful meadow. She took a deep breath, smelling the sweet scent of all the blooming flowers. There was a light breeze caressing her hair, and she could hear the faint melodic song of meadowlarks in the distance. It was something she had never experienced.

"Here's the place. It's one of my favorites on the ranch. I love to fish here or just listen to the stream and sit under the shade of the cottonwood trees. This is where…" Jarrod almost slipped again and said WHERE GRAYSON AND CHERYL GOT MARRIED.

"Where what?"

"Uh, this is just where I like to come to clear my mind. That's all."

"It's a lovely spot."

Jarrod had thrown an extra blanket under the saddle with the hopes that Charlotte would sit with him. He took the blanket and spread it under a large cottonwood tree next to the stream.

"Do you always carry an extra blanket with you?"

"Only when I want to sit with a lovely young lady like yourself." Jarrod took her hand and guided her over to the blanket. "Please, madam, would you kindly sit with me on this here woolen blanket, chosen especially for you and your comfort?"

"Why thank you, sir. I do believe I will."

They both laughed and sat down together. The air was slightly cooler under the shade tree, especially by the cold-water stream. It babbled down through the rocks, creating a soothing sound that Charlotte had never heard before and especially enjoyed.

"The meadow is so beautiful and the stream so serene and comforting. I now know why this is one of your favorite places here. It would be mine too."

"It can be yours, too."

"I certainly will remember it, but I'll be leaving soon for Boston, remember?"

"But you don't have to."

"I can't live in a hotel in Laurel Springs forever. I have to get on with my life. I don't have any reason to stay here. At least in Boston, I still have some family, my Aunt and Uncle, and I know I can find a job. What would I do here?"

"Be with me."

"Be with you? What do you mean?"

"Oh, Charlotte. I knew there was something special about you the first time I saw you. No one as beautiful as you has ever been to this town."

"What about my sister? Remember? She's my twin. She looks just like me."

"Yeah, but I knew from the start she was Grayson's so I never looked at her that way. Besides that, and don't tell her or Grayson this, but I think you're much prettier anyway."

"Flattery might not work this time, Jarrod. And how could you possibly know you want to be with me? We just met. We've only had a couple meals together."

"Oh, I know. But I can get to know you better if you would just stay. And you could get to know me. It's not like I'm asking you to marry me. I just want you to stay so we can know if it we were meant to be. I would have to chase you to Boston if you don't."

"Really? You would follow me all the way to Boston?"

"Yes, I would."

Charlotte liked Jarrod, but she wasn't sure she wanted to be in a courtship with him, especially so soon after Grayson.

"I am flattered by your interest in me, Jarrod, but I cannot make such a decision so soon. I need more time to think about things. I need to go back to Boston, by myself."

"Please, don't. What do I need to do to convince you?"

"You have been near perfect, aside from that crazy gallop ride you just took me on. I mean what I said about you. You are a gentleman whom any woman would be foolish to turn down."

"Then why are you?"

"Because I don't have those feelings right now for you. My heart won't allow it yet. Let me go back to Boston and think things through. I will write to you, and I hope you will write back. And then, if it's right, I will return to Laurel Springs and Wind River Ranch when my heart can be yours and only yours."

Jarrod was disappointed by her words, but didn't want to push her any further. "Okay, Charlotte. If that's how it must be."

"Yes, it must. I'm sorry."

"No need to be sorry. I'll be here waiting for you when you return."

"You're confidence is uncanny."

"It's my best attribute."

"One of them." Charlotte smiled and grabbed his arm. He lifted her up from the blanket and they returned in a slow walk on Clover back to the barn.

***

When they got back to the barn, Jarrod invited Charlotte to stay for dinner, but she declined. She just wanted to have one last conversation with Cheryl before she left on the stage tomorrow morning. Charlotte waited on the porch while Jarrod went inside to get Cheryl.

"Hi, Charlotte. I'm glad you wanted to talk again." Cheryl sat down in the chair next to her sister.

"I'm leaving tomorrow so I just wanted to see you before I left. I need to say this without interruption, so please bear with me." Cheryl nodded.

"I have decided that I must forgive you. I cannot bear this anger and carry it with me from now until eternity. You are my sister, and I love you. As twins, we share a bond that should never be broken. And as I said before, I cannot forget what you did, but I will learn to accept it in due time. I did not want to leave without you knowing this. I want to still communicate with you through letters. I want to know how you're doing and how your new baby is. I wish you and Grayson all the best and I hope one day we can all sit down and break bread together as a family, but it is not today. I wish you well, my sister." Charlotte stood up to offer Cheryl a hug.

"I love you, Charlotte. God bless you." Cheryl hugged her sister and they both cried.

"I love you too, Cheryl. I need to go now."

"I thought you might stay. I thought Jarrod would ask you to."

"He did, but I am not ready to stay. I need to return to Boston."

"But when will I see you again?"

"In due time. Goodbye, Cheryl."

"Goodbye, Charlotte."

Charlotte called over to Jarrod, who was out at the barn. She wanted to leave and not have to see or speak to Grayson.

Jarrod jogged over to the buggy where Charlotte was already seated. "Ready?"

"Yes, let's go please." Jarrod pulled the buggy away from the cabin as Cheryl gave Charlotte a final wave goodbye. Charlotte waved back and then quickly looked forward as she saw Grayson out of the corner of her eye, coming from the far pasture on his horse. "Can you go any faster?"

"Oh sure, now you want to go faster?"

"Yes, please!"

Jarrod just then saw Grayson and understood now why Charlotte was in such a hurry. He whipped the reins a few times, and they disappeared quickly out of sight, leaving behind only a dust trail by the time Grayson arrived at the house.

CHAPTER FOURTEEN

Almost a year had passed since Charlotte left Laurel Springs and returned to Boston. Since then, Cheryl had given birth to her baby boy, Michael.

Cheryl and Jarrod did keep in contact with Charlotte through letters. Jarrod had asked in nearly every one for her to return, but Charlotte always replied that she wasn't ready yet.

Because they had more time to correspond and because she had already met Jarrod in person, she felt more close to him than she ever did while corresponding to Grayson. But she just didn't want to rush into anything this time.

Charlotte did desire a husband and wanted to have a family, but wanted to make sure Jarrod was the right one. She didn't want to choose him by default. And she wanted to make sure she could be part of his family, alongside Grayson and Cheryl, without having any regretful feelings.

The entire time Jarrod wrote to Charlotte, he not once thought about being with any other women. Jarrod was handsome and wealthy, so there was never a shortage of women who were interested in him. But he was only interested in his lovely Charlotte who, unfortunately, was thousands of miles away.

Jarrod thought about going to Boston to be with her and convince her to return with him, but he knew he couldn't force her to do anything she didn't want to. He also knew he couldn't live in a city, so he would just have to wait for her to return to him. He never gave up hope that she would. In fact, not long after Charlotte left, he began to build a separate cabin on the ranch for them.

Grayson trotted up on his horse to find Jarrod putting the last few shingles on the roof. "Looks like it's almost finished."

"Yep. Do you think Charlotte will like it?"

"Of course. But she still hasn't said anything to you about coming back, has she?"

"No. Not yet. But she will."

"You're confident about that, aren't you?"

"It's one of my best traits, you know. Charlotte even said so."

"Well, if nothing else, you have a nice place to sleep until she comes back. Better than that old shack you had before."

"Yeah. It will be nice to have my very own place again. Now I don't have to be so careful and clean and be in Cheryl's way over in the main house. I can kick my boots off wherever I like."

"I'm sure both Cheryl and Miss Jean will appreciate that. Heck, I think I will too."

"Ha. Ha. And I love Jenni and Michael, but sometimes I just want to snooze, and it's hard with young'uns running all over the house. But hey, I'm still coming over for meals."

"Yeah, I figured that much."

"Well, Cheryl and Miss Jean are cooking meals anyway for you and the kids, so it's no big deal if I eat with y'all too."

"No. No it isn't. Aside from having to add another pound of food to the pot for you."

"I think I earn my keep here. Remember, besides you I also help raise all this beef around here."

"Just kidding you, brother. Of course you do. And I do hope one day that Charlotte returns. Sounds like she has your heart."

"She does. She's the only one for me."

"I'm happy that you feel like that about a woman. For awhile there, I thought you never would again. It's kind of weird to me, it being Charlotte and all, but if she's the one that'll make you happy, then I'll accept that and be happy for you."

"I know it's weird. But I figure after awhile, we'd all get over it. I reckon me and you have the same taste in woman, us both liking twin sisters and all."

"I guess it's kind of special. Two brothers marry two sisters."

"Well, I hope I get the chance to marry her. First I need to convince her to leave that wicked city of Boston."

"I don't see, after being out in this beautiful country of ours, how someone could want to live in a crowded, dirty city like that. Just keep writing the right words to her, have faith and in due time she'll just have to come back to you."

"I hope and pray everyday."

"Well, I'll see you later. I gotta go to town to pick up some things for Cheryl and the baby. You need anything?"

"Just Charlotte."

"If it was that easy, I'd bring her home for you."

"Yeah, I know. Naw. I don't need anything. But can you stop by the post office and see if there are any letters for me?"

"Will do." Grayson turned Buck around and headed back down the trail into town.

Every time Jarrod galloped through the meadow down to the stream, all he could think about was Charlotte. He always liked to go down there and fish, but the place was even more special now since he had memories of her being there with him.

As he got to the top of the hill and could see across the flowering field to the stream, he noticed something different. He could make out a figure down under the cottonwoods by the creek, but it was too far away to see who it was. He trotted a little faster until finally he could see it was a woman sitting on a blanket.

He could see the long, blonde hair draped over the back of her shoulders. Then she turned to look towards him and stood up. Jarrod instantly knew it was Charlotte. His lovely Charlotte had returned.

She waved to him in the distance, and he waved back. Jarrod galloped as fast as he could until he reached her. He stopped short and in one continuous motion, swung off the horse and then grabbed

Charlotte and swung her around in the air. "You're here! You're here! I just knew you would come back. But why didn't you tell me? How did you get here?"

"I just woke up one morning and realized I wanted to be with you in Laurel Springs more than by myself in Boston. I got on a train that afternoon, and here I am. A few days into the trip I was beginning to doubt my decision. Not about wanting to be with you, but not telling you or asking you ahead of time through a letter. I wondered, what if I show up and you changed your mind?"

"Not one moment since you left have I NOT wanted you to return. I'm so happy you did. But how did you get here, to the ranch and here next to the river?"

"I stayed at the hotel the first night. The next morning, Sid told me Grayson was at the blacksmith's, getting new shoes made for Buck. He was surprised to see me too, but gladly offered me a ride back to the ranch. He said you were out moving cattle to the upper grazing area and wouldn't be back for awhile. So I asked him to bring me down here so I could surprise you...Surprise!"

"You certainly did surprise me. I thought it was funny Grayson telling me to come down here. He made up some story about seeing a stray cow and its calf going over the hill this way and for me to go and fetch them back. He said he couldn't do it himself 'cause he had to help Cheryl with something. It sure was a nice surprise to find you here instead of a couple of cows."

"Well, I hope so. I know you and Grayson love your cattle, but I hope you love, or will love, me more."

"I certainly do. I do love you Charlotte."

"I love you too, Jarrod."

The two embraced. They didn't let go, but slowly pulled back from each other and gazed into each other's eyes. Jarrod moved in closer and then gave Charlotte a light, gentle kiss. "Charlotte, I know there is no other woman I would want to be with than you. I wasn't prepared for you to be here today or to ask this question, but it only feels right." Jarrod got down on his knee and held Charlotte's hands. "Miss Charlotte Abbey Chadwick, will you marry me?"

Charlotte was stunned. "I…I was not expecting this at all."

"Well, will you?"

Charlotte paused, looked at Jarrod and then quickly shook her head up and down. "Yes!"

Jarrod stood up and gave Charlotte another big hug and kiss. "I'm sorry I don't have a ring for you right now. Like I said, I didn't know I was gonna ask you. But I'll get you one right away. Anything you want."

"Oh, don't worry about that. A ring is not as important as your words and intentions right now. I want to marry you for who you are, not because of a ring."

"My Charlotte, that's why I love you so much! Now let's get back to the cabin and let everyone know." Jarrod helped Charlotte up on Clover.

"This time I wore appropriate under garments so I can sit astride." She swung one of her legs over the other side of the saddle. "But that doesn't mean you can take us into a full gallop again!"

Jarrod hopped onto Clover behind her, put his chin on Charlotte's shoulder as he reached around to grab the reins and softly said, "Whatever you say, dear." He kissed her on the cheek and then guided the horse back to the barn in a slow, reasonable gallop.

***

Jarrod and Charlotte walked up to the porch of the cabin where Miss Jean was sitting on the rocking chair.

"C'mon on in, Miss Jean. We have something to tell you and Grayson and Cheryl."

"Can't you just tell me without me having to get up?"

"Okay. Wait here, and I'll get Grayson and Cheryl to come out."

"That's sounds better to me and my knees."

Jarrod opened the door to the cabin and yelled for Grayson and Cheryl, "Hey, y'all, come on out. I got something to tell you."

"What?" Grayson yelled down to Jarrod from upstairs.

"Would you just come on out?"

"Alright. Alright."

"I need to come too?"

"Yeah, Cheryl. You too."

Grayson and Cheryl came out on the porch and saw Charlotte standing there next to Miss Jean. Grayson knew she was here, but hadn't told Cheryl. He wanted it to be a surprise for her too.

"Charlotte! What are you doing here?" Cheryl immediately gave Charlotte a big hug.

"I'll tell you everything, but first I think Jarrod has something he wants to say first."

"Uh, yes. Well..." Jarrod moved next to Charlotte and wrapped his arm around her. "Well, I wanted y'all to know that I asked Miss Charlotte to marry me and she said yes."

"Oh, that's wonderful!" Cheryl shouted out.

"Congratulations, little brother." Grayson shook Jarrod's hand and patted him on the back.

"Well it's about time." Miss Jean stayed sitting in her rocking chair and addressed Charlotte, "All this boy would ever talk about is you. He was beginning to mope around here like a sick puppy. Thank goodness you came back. I just about couldn't stand it no more, his love sickness and all."

Charlotte reached down to give Miss Jean a hug. "Well, I'm glad I could fix what ailed him, for his and your sake."

Everyone laughed. "Have you shown Charlotte her surprise?" Grayson asked Jarrod.

"No. Not yet."

"Surprise? Asking me to marry you was enough of a surprise. What else could you possibly have?"

"Come with me and I'll show you." Jarrod took Charlotte down the steps of the porch and into the wagon. He turned back to everyone who was still on the porch and yelled out, "We'll see y'all later."

***

Jarrod stopped the wagon before they ascended over the last hill where the new cabin was.

"Why did you stop?"

"We're getting close, and I want to put a blindfold on you so you can't see 'till we get there."

"My heavens. You really want this to be a surprise, don't you?"

"Yes. Now let me put this on you." Jarrod took his bandanna and wrapped it tightly around Charlotte's eyes. Then he waved his hands in front of her face. "You can't see anything, can you?"

"No. Not a thing."

"Good." They proceeded down the road until they got to the cabin. He guided her off the wagon and walked her up to the front of the house. "Ready?"

"Yes already!"

Jarrod took the blindfold off. Charlotte looked at the house, but didn't know what to think.

"How do you like it?"

"Whose cabin is this?"

"Ours!"

"Ours?"

"I started building it not long after you left. It's been kind of a slow process 'cause I only could work on it in my spare time, but I finally finished it last week. I'm so glad it was finished before you came."

"Oh, Jarrod. It's beautiful. Just beautiful. I can't believe you built this for me."

"It's for you, me and our family to be."

"This is just perfect. I never had my very own home. How kind of you. It's more than I could have ever imagined."

"I was hoping you would like it."

"More than like. I love it! But why did you build it? You didn't even know I would return."

"I knew you would come back to me. It was written in the stars that night we sat together and gazed at the sparkling sky. I knew in my heart that very moment you were mine to love for the rest of my life."

"I think I knew it too. It just took me longer to figure it out."

"I'm sure glad you did, otherwise I'd sure be lonely in this big house all by myself. I'd probably starve too. I'm hoping you can cook."

"I can, and I will cook you lots of meals in this house, as long as you're hungry."

"No problem there. Not at all. And I promise you I'll never be late for dinner."

"I'll keep you to that promise, among others."

"Yes, Ma'am!" Jarrod picked Charlotte up and carried her up the porch stairs.

"Now wait! Don't carry me across that threshold yet. We've gotta wait until we're married."

"Well, alright." Jarrod put her down on her feet. "But don't you want to see inside?"

"Of course. If I walk in on my own, then that's okay."

Jarrod opened the door. "After you, Madam."

Charlotte walked into the spacious foyer. Her eyes got big. She couldn't believe how nice it looked inside, even without any furniture. "You did this all by yourself?"

"Grayson helped me here and there when he could. But I designed the layout all by myself."

"It's just beautiful. So beautiful."

Jarrod took her by the hand and guided her from room to room. "See, here's the kitchen… And here's our room… And this room is for the baby and the next baby…."

"It's just wonderful. I don't know what else to say." Charlotte gave Jarrod a big hug. Tears rolled down her cheeks.

"Hey, I hope those are happy tears." Jarrod gently wiped the tears from her cheeks with his thumb.

"Yes, very happy tears."

"Good. I don't ever want to see you cry."

CHAPTER FIFTEEN

Jarrod and Charlotte were married the next day at the church. They wanted a simple wedding. Only Grayson, Cheryl, Jenni, Michael and Miss Jean were present.

After the ceremony, Jarrod drove Charlotte and himself back to their cabin. "May I now carry you across the threshold, Mrs. Charlotte Lee?"

"Yes you may, my husband."

Jarrod lifted her up effortlessly and carried her into the cabin and eventually to the bedroom that night…

One month later, Charlotte was talking to Miss Jean on the porch when suddenly she ran back into the house and got sick.

"Miss Jean, I haven't been feeling so good lately. I've been dizzy, queasy and tired."

"Here we go again. Let's go see Doc Turner, but I've got a feeling that we don't need his diagnosis, dear."

"Why's that?"

"I think all you're gonna need is a dress with more belly room real soon. While we're in town, we might as well get some more yarn too."

"More belly room? And more yarn for knitting….? Oh!"

"That's right, dear."

Just then, Jarrod came in on his horse from rounding up the cattle. "I sure am hungry. Lunch ready yet?" Jarrod took off his hat and wiped the sweat from his brow.

"I need more yarn!" Charlotte ran over to Jarrod and gave him a big hug.

"More yarn?" Puzzled, Jarrod leaned back away from Charlotte with his hands around her waist to see her face. "What does that have to do with anything?"

"Don't you see?" Charlotte threw her arms up in the air. "More yarn! And a bigger dress!"

"Woman, you're talking nonsense. Miss Jean, what's she talking about?"

"I think she should tell you."

"Tell me what?"

"We're gonna have a baby!"

"Baby?" Jarrod looked at Miss Jean and then at Charlotte. "A baby...a baby! Yeehaw!" Jarrod wrapped his arms low around Charlotte's waist and lifted her up off the ground in a tight embrace.

***

Nine months later, Charlotte gave birth to a healthy baby girl. They named her Jeanine, after Miss Jean, who had passed away a few months earlier.

Charlotte cradled Jeanine in her arms as she sat on the blanket with Cheryl who was taking out the food from the basket. Michael, now almost two, crawled around on the blanket while Jenni, now five, picked wildflowers in the meadow. Grayson and Jarrod were down by the stream fishing.

"Could you ever have imagined us sitting here together in this beautiful meadow with our precious children and adoring husbands?"

"It would have been just a dream. We've come a long way since our Boston days," Charlotte sighed.

"Mom and Dad would have been proud."

"They are. I know they're looking and smiling down on us right now."

"We certainly didn't plan it this way. There are definitely easier ways, but I'm glad it all worked out between all of us."

Jeanine started to fuss, so Charlotte put her over her shoulder and patted her gently on the back. "Easier doesn't always mean better. It isn't easy giving birth, but the reward for doing it is worth all the pain in the world."

"Yes. Enduring pain has provided us with our husbands and our children... Wait, I don't know if that came out right?"

Charlotte laughed. "No, you're right. They're a pain sometimes."

"But worth every second of it. Speaking of..." Cheryl yelled over to the men, "Hey you two! Come and eat!"

Jarrod yelled back, "Alright! Just one more cast!"

"It's always just one more, isn't it?"

"Just one more kiss too. And that's why Jeanine is gonna have a baby sister or brother."

"Really? Congratulations!" Cheryl reached over and gave Charlotte a hug.

Grayson and Jarrod returned from the stream and sat down on the blanket, both giving a kiss on the cheek to their wives. Grayson picked up Michael and put him in his lap.

Jarrod rubbed his belly while looking at all the food. "I'm starving!"

"What else is new?" Charlotte reached over to give Jarrod a piece of chicken.

Cheryl yelled over to Jenni who was still picking flowers, "Jenni...Come on back. It's time to eat."

"Okay, Momma." Jenni came skipping back and gave the bouquet of daisies to Charlotte.

"For me?" Jenni nodded her head. "Thank you. How did you know that daisies were my favorite?"

"My mom told me. Just like your ring."

A month earlier, Cheryl had told Jarrod she wanted to give her daisy pattern ring to Charlotte, knowing it was really meant for her. Grayson understood, but Jarrod didn't want to give Grayson's ring to Charlotte as it was. To make it more special, he sent it back to Tiffany & Co. and asked that the center diamond be removed and replaced by a yellow diamond. So now the yellow center diamond was surrounded by the eight white diamond "petals" to form a perfect gem daisy.

Grayson had another ring made for Cheryl from the remaining center diamond. Cheryl said she didn't want anything more than the one diamond on her ring. It represented the joyful simplicity of her new life in the country and the only thing that mattered—her family.

Charlotte and Cheryl went down to the stream with the children while the men continued to eat on the blanket.

"Could you ever have imagined us being out here like this?" Grayson leaned back on the blanket and looked down towards the stream.

"Yeah, this chicken is so good."

"No, you numbskull." Grayson shook his head and struck Jarrod on the shoulder. "I mean here with our two beautiful wives and children."

"Oh, yeah. Right. Naw. I kind of just figured I would be fine being a lone cowboy, but then I met Charlotte and everything changed."

"Well, it wasn't easy getting to this point, but it sure was worth all the pain."

"Yeah, like when you hit your thumb with a hammer kind of pain." Jarrod lifted up his bruised thumb.

"Exactly. It isn't easy building a house. But the reward for doing it is worth all the pain in the world."

"Yeah." Jarrod shook his head. "Women don't even know all the pain we have to go through as men."

"I'm sure women have some kind of similar pain that's worth it too," Grayson replied.

"Like hammer-thumb pain?" Jarrod asked.

"They say childbirth isn't exactly a bowl full of cherries."

"Oh, yeah. I'm guessing childbirth is right up there with hammer-thumb pain." Jarrod looked down at his thumb again.

"Yeah, that's probably it."

They both chuckled and then grabbed another piece of chicken.

Grayson yelled to the women, "Hey ladies, come on back to the blanket with us."

"We'll be right there. Just one more minute," Cheryl replied.

"It's always one more minute, isn't it?"

"And always worth the wait, every time." Grayson smiled and Jarrod nodded in agreement.

Grayson, Cheryl, Jarrod and Charlotte sat on the blanket together with their children. They ate, talked and laughed as the warm, gentle breeze blew soft waves across the deep green meadow. The babbling stream in the background flowed constant, as did the love between the two families.

Miss Jean was right; EVERYTHING WASN'T GOING TO BE ALL NICE AND EASY WITH SMILES ALL THE TIME. But no matter what obstacles laid ahead, no matter what hardships they had to face, nothing would ever come between them again—because family always came first.

~The End~

The Next Story...

Mail Order Bride: Evergreen - A Sweet Western Historical Romance

Thank You!

I know you have lots of choices when it comes to books, so I'd like to **thank you** for choosing to read my story.

If you enjoyed *Love, Honor & Keep Her*, I'd be very grateful if you left a quick review on Amazon. I read every one and appreciate them very much.

Connect with Rose

I love meeting readers of my books. Stop by and say hello on my Facebook page:

https://www.facebook.com/rosedumontbooks

Or you can contact me through my email:
rosedumontbooks@gmail.com

Thanks again for reading my book. Hope you enjoyed it!

~Rose

Made in United States
Troutdale, OR
11/11/2024